Happy Ho~ ˙
to Nick
from Stan
a Christmas ~m~~
Crime Caper

INVITATION
TO A FEW
MURDERS

on page 138 in the
worst ever ~~parl~~ parody
of T. S. Eliot.

Stanley Reynolds

Grosvenor House
Publishing Limited

All rights reserved
Copyright © Stanley Reynolds, 2014

The right of Stanley Reynolds to be identified as the author of this
work has been asserted by him in accordance with Section 78
of the Copyright, Designs and Patents Act 1988

The book cover picture is copyright to Stanley Reynolds

This book is published by
Grosvenor House Publishing Ltd
28-30 High Street, Guildford, Surrey, GU1 3EL.
www.grosvenorhousepublishing.co.uk

This book is sold subject to the conditions that it shall not, by way of
trade or otherwise, be lent, resold, hired out or otherwise circulated
without the author's or publisher's prior consent in any form of binding or
cover other than that in which it is published and
without a similar condition including this condition being imposed
on the subsequent purchaser.

A CIP record for this book
is available from the British Library

ISBN 978-1-78148-749-5

Prologue

Mimi of the Movies someone called her. It was meant to be satirical. She wouldn't know about that.

"What's satire?" Mimi wanted to know. She was posing on a piece of sinful red velvet furniture in her naughty girlie bedroom. Golden California sunshine was streaming in through an open window.

"Satire?" said her new friend from last night. He couldn't believe how thick she was. But beautiful, and horny. "It's a sort of serious joke," he said.

"What's the point of that? I think you gotta take life as a joke or else you're gonna be miserable."

"You know," he said, "you're coming awfully close to quoting a German philosopher?"

Mimi believed what she said about life but her eyes were anxious and full of the memory of past frustrated greed.

"Cut the baloney," she said. She didn't sound really annoyed. Then she did. "I got places to go and people to see, so you can find where you flung your clothes last night and fling them back on."

He was someone who didn't matter. Of course, he might kill himself out of love for her, a love which she wasn't going to return. That'd be nice.

She flew out from LAX, heading East to New England for Christmas.

Nick was there in Boston to meet her.

Two sisters were riding in the back of Nick's station wagon. They were Vita and Margot Cuncliffe. She remembered she had met Margot, the redhead, before. They were kind of cousins of Nick's, the daughters of Nero Cuncliffe of Eastsodom, Long Island..

They were good-looking in expensive clothes. The sort of expensive clothes that only other women in expensive clothes recognized. Mimi considered that a waste of time and money. Their voices were also full of money. They were fashionable nobodies.

Nick asked them what they had been doing since they left college. They hadn't been doing anything. Except romance.

"What's he do?" Nick asked the redhead Margot of her latest lover.

"Just a prep school teacher. And school football coach."

"You better come into some money soon," Vita said.

"I intend to," Margot said.

They laughed. It was a joke. Money could be a joke with them because they always had it, Mimi thought.

She was in the front seat watching them in the rearview mirror.

"What's wrong with her?" she said to Nick.

Margot said, "Don't talk about me as if I weren't here. I just have some trouble with my nose. Now and then I like a little coke. It cuts down the boredom."

Then they started to talk about the rich good-looking college girls and boys they knew.

"How long have I got to sit here listening to this?" Mimi asked Nick.

"Five hours."

"You're kidding. Five hours. I'll kill myself. Or take to cocaine."

Once they were North of Boston there was snow by the side of the road. It grew deeper every mile they went until it was banked up higher than the car. Plows were out.

Donald Billings, Nick's best man, will be there, Mimi thought. That might mean some fun. She'd slept with him three or four times when Nick wasn't looking. Maybe he'd kill himself. It had happened before, it might happen again. You ain't no white trash no more, she told herself; you're Mimi of the Movies and there ain't no satire about that.

Crows as black as ink flew this way and that above the confusing white whirl of snow. One of them, the black ink blackest, was the devil getting ready to claim Mimi as one of his own. There was religion in these old Puritan hills.

1

And there was ten million dollars in the room but they tried to ignore it.

They didn't want to look eager. They all wanted to see the old man dead, but if they looked it he might cut them out of the Will. With an old man like Andrew Burgess you could never tell what he might do. He was eighty percent bastard; the other twenty percent was foul mood.

Old Andrew had a small town bankroll. There was now an empty mill in Holford that once belonged to him. Then there was the old house at the top of Memory Hill.

This was a party at Gledhill, the big old fashioned spook ridden house on a mountain slope on the way out of the rural New England township of North Holford.

If they sent out invitations to the party it should have said, Come To a Few Murders. RSVP to Old Edward Burgess or the even Older and Meaner Andrew Burgess.

Anyway, nobody was happy. It was Christmas and the room should be in Technicolor, but there were no decorations.

"Who built this place, Edgar Allan Poe?" said a girl who was so beautiful she ought to be in pictures.

"I dunno," said the fat man next to her, "I was just driving by."

"You mean you're not no member of no family?"

"Hell no, I stopped the car because of this old guy who looked lost and he invited me to a party."

"Which old guy?"

"That one over there."

He pointed across the room which was filling up with people.

"That's not the right old guy, that's his brother."

"Whose brother?"

"Andrew's brother. Andrew's the recluse who lives here."

"Sure, I know that. We all know Old Man Andrew Burgess, we just never see him much. He hides away up here."

After a moment for thought the fat boy said, "Well, whatever I'm here now. My name's Davy Shea."

"I'm Mimi Burgess," she said, "a Hollywood star."

"You married to one of them old guys?"

"No, I'm married to Nick Burgess, a nephew of those old guys. We came here for Christmas because he wants to get into Andrew's good books and come in for the loot when the old boy's carried away."

"And you don't want no dough?"

"Naw."

"What are you, one of them Hollywood broads who make millions?"

"Unfortunately not yet. But I will. I've had men kill themselves for me. Though so far they weren't anything important. One was a car mechanic in San Antonio and the other was a furniture salesman in Houston."

"Do only gents in Texas kill themselves for you?"

"I was in high school in Texas at the time. Now that I'm in the movies, I'll get plenty of publicity when they start killing themselves wholesale."

"Have I seen you in any pictures?"

"How would I know? Stick around though. I've got a DVD of my latest. You'll see me parading around in just exactly what you and the rest of the boys been longing for."

"The ladies I know get right down to it."

"What kind of ladies is they?"

"Mostly burger joint waitresses."

"How come that don't surprise me none? Never mind, I used to sling hash in a place you wouldn't take your mother to no matter how drunk she was. I'm genuine trailer trash; I've got the certificate."

"But you're in Hollywood."

"Sure thing, I got my ass out of Texas, or rather my ass got me out of Texas. I'm getting ahead and in my new movie I don't chew no gum and I don't take my pants off until page twelve."

"I don't know if I can stay for no feed," Davy said. "I'm not no real guest."

"Who is? We all been invited by Uncle Edward. Uncle Andrew don't invite nobody nowhere. It's like we all piled in uninvited into old Scrooge's place."

"Scrooge? I've heard that name. He's got something to do with Santa Claus, don't he?"

"In this case Scrooge is Santa Claus's brother."

"That's real interesting."

Davy met a few more guests. Two sisters, Vita and Margot Cuncliffe. Margot was a fireworks redhead; Vita was only reddish brown. They were tough babes that Bryn Mawr had produced - by mistake. But if Bryn Mawr started doing it in earnest the Cuncliffe sisters would be good role models. Vita and Margot looked down on Mimi and when they learned that Davy was a cop they felt free to look down on him too.

"If you're a policeman," Vita said, "where's your uniform?"

"I'm off duty today, but my gun's in the car."

"In case you have to shoot someone?"

"Unfortunately I haven't actually shot anyone, at least not shot them dead. I wounded one guy once."

"You must practice. There are a few people here you could practice on. Old Man Andrew Burgess doesn't move too quick. You could hit him. No one would feel bad about that, especially if they're mentioned in the Will."

Uncle Edward saw Davy and came across the room to him.

"Sergeant," he said, "could you help us put up the Christmas tree in the hall? Two of Andy's servants – staff I should say – cut one down and brought it in, but they've got other things to do."

"Can we help decorate it?" Margot said. She was being a wide-eyed kid full of the music of sleigh bells and six large whiskies.

Edward had been studying the three girls, wondering how they were able to wear such few clothes in the cold. The room wasn't heated. Andrew obviously hoped this would drive them away. It might possibly work, Edward thought. Mimi went out and came back looking like a beefed up odalisque wearing three sweaters. Margot Cuncliffe was rubbing her bare arms and shoulders. The beautiful Mimi was well padded. There was a touch of red showing above her green sweater. She looked like a rose bud enclosed in green leaf. She removed the green sweater and she was a bright red new rose. Then she removed that bright garment and the next was pink, like an Albertine grown old. Mimi gave two of her layers to Margot. Vita left the room and came back wearing a heavy coat. All the girls had the "tyranny of youth."

"Let's start on the tree," Margot said, "where are the decorations?"

Andrew heard her and he smiled as much as his face would permit and said, "I don't have any Christmas decorations in this house and never had any in any place I've ever lived in."

He was especially bad tempered because he was somewhat crippled. He was now doddering round leaning on two sticks. Occasionally he regretted having ignored the curvy girls of his youth who skipped between New York nightclubs and the sand of Palm Beach. Still, he had had only one million then; there was no time to waste.

He looked about and took in the disappointed faces of those who wanted a happy Yuletide.

He laughed, it was not a pleasant sound, especially issuing from the antediluvian face.

Edward also laughed, a real laugh. He was something of a jolly old soul.

"It's all right," Edward said. "I've brought decorations down with me. I've got strings of lights and colored balls to hang on the tree, and plenty of tinsel and a star to put on top of the tree."

"You've no right to do that," Andrew said.

"Don't mind Andrew," Edward said to the redheaded Margot, "he'll catch the Christmas spirit soon. I've got some carolers coming. That should do it."

Andrew didn't say anything but his face looked like he was about to say "humbug".

The two workmen who brought the tree in came back to see if there was anything else they could do.

"Hello Tom, hello Dick," Uncle Edward said. He spoke as if they were old pals.

"He's all right," Tom whispered to Dick.

"He's still the brother of the other one," Dick said.

"You mean if we knock off Old Andrew we'd have to eliminate the other too?" Tom said.

"Don't talk like that," Dick said. "Some day someone's bound to murder Andrew and we don't want no blame."

"The cops are going to have a tough time," Tom said. "Everyone wants to see him dead."

"Yeah," Dick said, "Police Chief Parker 'Boomer' Daniels is going to be up to the neck in suspects."

"Sergeant Davy Shea," Tom said, "what's he doing here? Maybe Boomer knows something's up and sent Shea."

Two more couples came in. One was middle-aged and the other in their twenties or early thirties.

The older ones were Stephen and Jane Hopkins, the Burgess brothers' late sister was Stephen's mother. The younger couple were Jack and Ottoline Smith. Jack was a distant cousin.

A lone figure wearing a tweed jacket and dark gray flannel trousers came in. No one seemed to know him. He turned out to be Bruce Dane, who wanted to buy the house but Andrew wouldn't sell. He was another of Edward's surprise visitors. There was something amusing about Dane's hair. It seemed to have slipped down one side of his forehead, like a hat that was tilted. It was an ill-fitting rug.

Then another local came into the room. This was Dr Phyllis Skypeck. She was not dressed fashionably but she was pretty enough with blue eyes and dark hair to look good in anything.

Mimi Burgess saw Phyllis and with perhaps a kindred feeling of one beautiful woman for another, came across the room and introduced herself. She then pointed out other members of the family.

"I know Andrew Burgess," Phyllis said. "I came here the other day to see Mr Andrew Burgess."

"I hope it was nothing bad; just uncomfortable."

"I can't tell you about patients of mine," Phyllis said.

"So long as Uncle Andrew isn't going to drop down dead and force me to live here. My husband, Nick, is his heir and Nick loves this house and all that lousy New England countryside that gives me the heebee geebees."

They went into lunch. Andrew Burgess looked at them as if they were stealing the food.

Edward Burgess tried to cheer up the scene talking about the DVD of Mimi's latest movie which they were going to see in the library later.

He suddenly looked troubled and said, "But how wise will it be showing herself as an actress? Andrew doesn't like actors. He won't think she is fit to give him a grandson to carry on his name."

Uncle Andrew suddenly said, "I'm going to change my Will."

"That's giving all of us a reason for murder this Christmas," Margot said.

It was meant to be a joke but no one laughed or even smiled.

"Well, here's the movie," Mimi said.

"Is it a murder or about doctors?" someone said.

"Neither," Mimi said, "it's about sex."

And the first scene showed her naked.

"That should please you, Uncle Andrew, those are good childbearing hips," Jane Hopkins said.

"The breasts grow enormous in pregnancy," Vita said, "and those are big enough already. Are they real Mimi?"

Mimi didn't answer.

On the screen she was body and bone naked pretending afternoon lust on rose petal sheets with Burt Emery, a muscular Hollywood stud. "He broke into the big time after playing a pansy in porn," Mimi said.

"Whatever are your children going to say when they see this?" Uncle Edward said.

But there were loads of laughs laid on by a famed character-actor, Billy Lee Lawson, playing Max Jerkoffsky, who made sure everyone knew this was daring comedy by the repeated use of one naughty ten-letter word and one vile twelve-letter one. Our Saviour was given a middle initial that was uttered in tight corners.

"Jee-zuzz H. Christ," the outgoing Max Jerkoffsky cried stumbling upon Mimi and Burt in one sex scene. Candy Ass O'Brien, the girl next door, was played by Dixie Smith, a real redhead it was proved, who was once at the local summer stock theater. She wisecracked and endlessly popped bubblegum.

All eyes, however, were on Mimi in the altogether.

"My God!" cried Nick Burgess, blushing crimson.

"Leaping lizards!" Vita Cuncliffe said, "a panther woman."

"Them panties," Davy said, considering an Xmas gift for Sadie Thompson, a waitress at the Puritan Maid Diner, "is them expensive panties?"

"Them ain't real," the movie star said, "they was sewed on me." Blushing, with shy downcast eyes, she added, "By a lady, with warm hands."

"I find it dreadful," Nick said, "simply awful."

"But it is amusing," Jane said, "the future heiress showing her bare ass to the world."

"Unless that's a stand-in ass," Vita said. "They have them. Can you imagine saying your occupation is being Mimi Burgess's ass."

"And someone else plays the tits?" Jane said.

"I wish somebody else would do the whole thing," Nick said.

"He's real worried about that Will being changed," Ottoline Smith whispered to her husband, Jack.

"Is there much more of it?" Uncle Andrew suddenly said.

"Just over an hour," Mimi said.

"Is it all just fornication?"

"There's some more with Burt Emery and then he beats me up because he finds out I've been humping with a few guys."

"Can you skip through to where he beats you up," Jane said.

Uncle Andrew got up and left.

"He's gone to change his Will," someone said.

The rest of the movie was not a success.

When they were all leaving the library Nick Burgess was heard saying to Mimi,"I wonder what you think you achieved showing that."

And then Phyllis Skypeck said to Davy Shea, "It looks like snow out there."

Through the window they could see snow starting to fall.

Phyllis said, "We'll be busy with people hurt in car crashes or just falling down on the ice; and, of course, the way things are shaping up here there might be a good old-fashioned Christmas murder."

2

Snow did come in the night, quite heavy snow.

There were kids out on sleds early in the morning and on the side of the mountain that hovered over North Holford skiers were also out.

The snow-making machine that had been making much noise and little snow the week before was now silent. Parker Daniels was outside his station shoveling snow off the sidewalk even though it was still snowing.

Sergeant Davy Shea pointed this out to him.

"Well," Parker said, "it'll mean there will be less to shovel when it does stop."

Davy went back into the station to drink coffee and eat doughnuts. Somewhere he had been told real policemen ate doughnuts and he had taken up the hobby.

He had also heard, and seen in the movies and on TV, that real policemen shot people. Davy's failure to shoot anyone successfully troubled him.

Parker Daniels had killed some bad guys, who had been trying to kill him, and this seemed unfair to Davy because Parker really didn't like killing them.

The part about the bad guys shooting at you wasn't so good, Davy thought. He decided to have another doughnut and wonder what the snow would do to the football. The New York Jets were playing the New England Patriots on Sunday. Davy liked football almost as much as he liked doughnuts, shooting people and baseball.

In the Spring baseball would come. The Boston Red Sox was his team. But it was snowing right now and the Boys of Summer seemed a long way off.

When the telephone rang he had to put down another doughnut to answer it.

After he answered it he ran outside to tell Parker.

"Boomer," he said, "there's been a shooting up at Andrew Burgess's house. I was there yesterday, right on the spot but nobody bothered to shoot no one."

"That's pretty inconsiderate of them," Parker said. "Who did get shot?"

"I told you nobody got himself shot."

"Not yesterday. Today."

"They weren't too clear. They was kind of hysterical. But it must have been Old Man Andrew. He's the one with the bucks and the Will which he was saying yesterday that he was going to change and cut people out of it."

"We better get up there. Is Georgie Stover coming in this morning?"

"He should be here any moment," Davy said. The moment came. Georgie entered.

The snow plows were out on the main street that ran alongside the old village green, they went past the police station and on down to the College Inn. The plows made a pleasant sound; there was nothing to fear and soon it would be Christmas.

Once out of town it was different. No plows had been there and it was difficult driving.

When they came to the house at the top of Memory Hill they saw that someone had made a snowman on the lawn.

They started walking to the house when another car pulled up and Dr Phyllis Skypeck got out.

"You doing this one?" Davy said. "Where's Stanley Howes, drunk again?"

Dr Howes was the medical examiner. Phyllis took his place when he couldn't make it.

"I almost stayed here last night," Phyllis said, "except Ottoline Smith took exception to the idea."

"Who's Ottoline Smith?" Parker asked.

"Jack Smith's wife."

Although Parker once thought that Phyllis and he would become an item Phyllis had made herself an item with so many others that Parker got the idea that he and Phyllis would never make it.

I suppose I'm too old for her, he thought. And I've been married and divorced and I have two daughters. He thought he wasn't much of a catch.

He rang the bell and the door was opened right away.

It was the sort of a house where you might think a butler would block the doorway.

Instead it was Edward Burgess.

"This is terrible," he said, "calling you out in this snow storm for a murder."

"I'm not that surprised," Davy said, "the way Andrew Burgess was talking yesterday about changing his Will."

"It's not Andrew," Edward said, "it's Nick Burgess, our nephew. He was shot dead."

"Where is he?" Parker said.

"In the back."

"He was shot in the back?" Davy said.

"No, I mean the body's in the back."

He led them to an extension that was called the garden-room. It had an orange tree and a banana tree. It also contained a tennis net, a number of racquets, all of them quite old wooden ones in frames. There were skis and ski poles and ski boots.

The garden-room also contained the dead body of Nick Burgess.

Phyllis got down and started examining him.

"He was shot in the heart at very close range," she said.

"By someone he obviously knew," Davy said.

"When did it happen?" Parker said.

"Sometime this morning?" Phyllis said. "I'll know after the autopsy. Will you want to come to it?" she added.

This was a joke. She knew what Parker was like. He'd faint if he saw her opening a corpse.

"I'll have to take a rain check," Parker said.

Then he saw Edward Burgess standing there and he thought their remarks might be in bad taste. He said, "Has his wife been informed?"

"Not yet," Edward said.

"We'd better go up and tell her," Parker said.

There were two staircases to the upper floors. Parker took the one that was obviously the servants'.

Well, he said to himself, I reckon we are servants.

It was embarrassing anyway to be in a big house like Gledhill, a house with a name instead of a street number. He imagined it was also full of rich and possibly important people. They were always difficult.

Davy must have been thinking the same thing because he said, "Down in Brazil and them places they take suspects to the basement facilities and belt them around until they get the idea."

"I don't think they do that to the rich," Parker said. "I think the poor are the ones they can torture. I think they even write down the ones who can be tortured."

The highly attractive Mimi Burgess was in her room.

She looked like she hadn't heard about the murder.

She gave them a big smile. She even threw her long hair back in a flirtatious manner and did something so her sweater slid off one shoulder.

This meant nothing to Parker but Davy had seen many movies and TV dramas and knew this was what beautiful young women did just in case you hadn't noticed how beautiful and young they were.

Davy reckoned that when Mimi Burgess got up and walked around they might get another show. But, he thought, by that time she'll have heard of her husband's murder and wouldn't walk in no entertaining way. Still, she had nice long legs and he could look at them.

Parker's eyes were also busy.

He was attempting to see if there was any evidence of Mimi Burgess having left the room, possibly even gone outside.

She said she hadn't.

She got up and walked a few steps and then sat down on the bed as if her legs had given away.

She was bent over, biting her lip. There were tears in her eyes and they started running down her face.

She's an actress, of course, Parker thought.

Then he saw that she was barefoot. There was something odd about that.

"Your husband was going skiing?" Davy said. "Do you ski?"

There were a pair of ski boots on the floor.

Parker picked one boot up.

He thought he might have something there, but he said, "I guess we can let you alone, Mrs Burgess. We've got plenty of others to see."

"Yeah," Davy said, "the house is bulging with suspects."

*

They wanted to start with Andrew Burgess but he wasn't available.

"Oh, bring anyone in," Parker said.

The first one was Jack Smith, the man Phyllis said she was interested in.

Jack looked like an athlete, not tremendously big like someone who played for Michigan or Notre Dame but like a running back for some small classy college like Harvard, Princeton or Yale.

Parker had worked in a law office in Boston and it was full of Harvardmen. Parker had been there because he was married to the boss's daughter. She left him, ran away from Parker and from the two girls who were very young then. Parker could have stayed on in the Boston firm but he knew that was because his father-in-law was sorry for him.

Parker came back home to North Holford with his daughters. He tried to be a lawyer but there wasn't enough work in a small town for the lawyers who were already there.

Then the Mayor saved him by making him the police chief.

Jack Smith looked at Parker and he thought he was a rube cop who hadn't been to an expensive school and was probably poor.

Davy didn't take to Jack Smith.

"You a college boy?" he said.

"I used to be."

"Yeah, where was that at?"

"Amherst."

"I don't know if that has anything to do with the murder," Parker said.

"College boys," Davy said, "they think they can get away with anything."

"Well," Jack Smith said, "I may have been a college boy but I don't have any money. I'm in real estate in Rhode Island and you know how bad business is now."

"Where were you this morning?" Parker said.

"I went skiing."

"Did you see Nick Burgess?"

"No, I must have left before he came down to go skiing."

"How'd you know he was going out skiing?" Davy said.

"Somebody told me."

"Or you know because you shot him dead," Davy said. "Where's your gun now?"

"I don't have a gun. Except a shotgun for when I go skeet shooting."

Davy didn't like the idea of skeet shooting. It was another rich man's sport. The only good thing he could say about it was that it wasn't played on horses.

"What about this wife of yours? Maybe she shot him. What's her name? Gladys or Doris?"

Parker almost smiled at the way Davy was bugging Jack Smith, coming up with two good working class names like Gladys and Doris.

"Ottoline, her name is Ottoline."

"That's a foreign name ain't it? Are we going to need someone to put into American anything she says when we're grilling her?"

"She is foreign but she's English."

"That's OK then, they speak American pretty good over there."

Davy was out doing himself, Parker thought, but it was the holiday season and Davy should be allowed to have some fun.

When Jack Smith left Parker said, "We're going to be here all day and night, Davy. You better go out and snoop around with the people who work here and see what's what with them."

"One of them could have done it," Davy said.

"That's why I'm sending you, but don't think you can torture them just because they're working stiffs, this isn't Brazil, not yet at least."

Parker had Edward come in.

He was surprised at how nervous Edward became when he was asked where he was at the time of the murder.

Then Edward said, "I suppose this is going to ruin Christmas."

"That's entirely up to you," Parker said. "You're going to have to eat so you might as well all sit down together and eat turkey."

"That's true," Edward said and seemed relieved. He had nothing to say.

Then Vita Cuncliffe came in wearing next to nothing. She was chilly enough to keep rubbing her bare arms.

Parker wondered if he should offer her his coat.

He didn't think it was the sort of thing real policemen were supposed to do. Then he gave her his coat.

Vita was still in bed when the murder was committed.

"Staying in bed was the warmest place I could be, even being alone in bed."

She looked up at Parker as if she had said something terribly original.

The flame haired Margot Cuncliffe came in next, also wearing hardly anything. She rubbed her bare arms but Parker did not offer her his coat.

She had been in bed when Nick Burgess was shot, but she had not been alone. Stephen Hopkins had been with her.

"But he wasn't there all night," she said, "he could have got up and killed Nick."

"I thought Stephen Hopkins was a middle-aged man," Parker said.

"He is, that's why he left early."

When Stephen Hopkins came in he turned out to be a good-looking man with no gray in his hair. He was very well dressed in a tweed suit that fit him as though tailor made.

"I'm told," Parker said, "that you don't have an alibi for the time of the murder."

"That Cuncliffe bitch told you, I'm not surprised. I was told she was a little whore."

"A whore? Did you pay her?"

"Certainly not. I've never had to pay a woman, and even if I wanted to I haven't the money now. The bottom's dropped out of the market."

"I suppose you hope to get something out of Andrew Burgess."

"I hope so. Of course in this era of everyday billionaires, and ordinary just millionaires sitting at street corners asking for spare change, Old Andrew's stash ain't much, but it'll do for now."

Jane Hopkins came in next.

Parker had expected a poor hard done woman, but Jane Hopkins was no victim. At least she didn't look like one.

She was as tailor-made as her husband and when she spoke she sounded tremendously sure of herself. It was, Parker thought, an odd way for poor people to act. I guess, he said to himself, they haven't got used to being poor yet.

Jane Hopkins said, "I was alone most of the night until he tried to creep back unnoticed. He might have had time to kill poor Nick Burgess."

"I'll keep that in mind."

After the Hopkins woman they finally got to Andrew.

The bad tempered millionaire didn't seem upset by his nephew's death.

"Of course it's a shame to lose my principal heir, but I like to think how much this has spoiled Christmas for that fool of a brother of mine and all those useless people cluttering up my house and eating and drinking at my expense. Every cloud has a silver lining – so they say but I don't know why it should."

"You'll have to put up with the visitors until we've solved the crime."

That hurt the old man. He winced.

The odd face, like a turtle's poked out from its shell, was from the days before Noah's Flood.

3

Davy questioned Tom and Dick, the yardmen, and Doris, the cook, and the various women and girls who came to the house every day from their homes in North Holford.

Davy and Parker knew them all.

"Anyone of them could have killed him," Davy said.

"And are they the sort of folks who possess pistols?"

"Pistols?" Pistol seemed an old-fashioned word to him. He liked the word handgun.

"I mean a revolver or an automatic," Parker said. "They are very expensive. Also you can't just buy them in this state. You need a permit."

"Well, maybe they saved up. Or they stole one."

"Or they happened to find it. I rather like the idea of that. Having found a gun they wondered who they could possibly shoot with it."

Whimsy, Davy thought, Parker's coming down with whimsy again.

Dr Phyllis Skypeck came in.

"I've got patients I've got to see in town," she said. "I hope these people have finished killing each other."

Parker let Phyllis go.

"It was well known that the late Nick liked this house, and Mimi didn't," Davy said. "Maybe she shot him so she wouldn't have to live here."

Davy didn't think much of Boomer's questions. For example, Boomer wanted to know who built the snowman.

No one knew who had made it.

"Well, Davy," Parker said, "Old Man Andrew Burgess is having a lot of fun with his nephew's death. I wonder how many other people will have to be murdered to keep him in the holiday spirit?"

A little later on when they were eating sandwiches and drinking beer in the Puritan Maid Diner in North Holford Davy said, "I know for a fact that lackadaisical attitude of yours put off the clients when you was trying to be a lawyer here. I suppose it was the same thing in Boston."

"No," Parker said, "my trouble in Boston was being a lackadaisical husband."

They went back to the house where Edward Burgess was pretending again that he was the host.

"Shouldn't you get the State Police in on this?" he said. "They've got the men and the money. And all the latest technical stuff."

"Well," Parker said, "maybe we could call them in later on. Along with the C.I.A. and the F.B.I., and the rest of the gangbusters."

This seemed to make Edward even more doubtful about Parker's abilities.

"What are we going to do, Boomer?" Davy asked.

They were in the library. There was a log fire and adding to the coziness they had a good view of the lawn and the fields beyond it buried in snow.

Davy was just about to say he was tired of talking to the same people when Edward informed them that more Christmas visitors were coming.

"They're coming in spite of the murder?" Parker said.

"I don't think they know about it," Edward said.

"Margot's friend Bill Summers is coming," Edward said.

"Who's the other new person?" Parker asked.

"Donald Billings," Edward said, "a friend of Nick's."

✻

At that time Donald Billings was driving to North Holford.

He met the snow alongside the Connecticut River just before he came to Northampton, Massachusetts.

He knew this town from years before when he was dating a girl at Smith College. He knew the other side of the river too where there had been a girl at Mount Holyoke College.

They ruined a lot of weekends for me, he thought. I'd have done myself a favor if I'd stayed away from them. Of course I didn't know that at the time. You never do. I wouldn't have two ex-wives if I did. Or be going to North Holford.

✻

Not far away from North Holford someone else was thinking of the Cuncliffe sisters, particularly of Margot.

This was Bill Summers. He taught history at Cheshire Academy in the pretty New England town of East Cheshire.

He didn't want to spend Christmas at the Burgess house. I want to go to New York, he said to himself. I spend my entire life looking at grass and trees and I want to be in a city.

He thought fondly of the heavy traffic in the New York streets, and the tall buildings. He could go there now if he wasn't going to North Holford. He could go but he wouldn't be able to afford much of a good time. Teaching at a prep school wasn't well paid. At a rich school like Cheshire the boys and girls came from wealthy families and looked down on the poorly paid teachers. The students' pet name for him was Big Bad Bill; they knew of his sex life.

Cheshire Academy would become only a bad dream when he married Margot. She would get money when Andrew Burgess passed away. Especially now Nick was dead.

He began to wonder how soon Andrew Burgess would be polite enough to die.

Andrew was only seventy-eight or nine, at least not yet eighty, but his health was bad. He had had a heart attack, and something mysterious was wrong with his legs. He shuffled about, keeping up-right on two sticks. He tried not to do it in front of anyone.

That was why he sat alone in his room or in the library for most of the day. Margot told Bill how Andrew was being more than usually bad tempered.

4

Mimi Burgess stood in her room looking out at the snow.

She could see the snowman looking lonely, looking in fact rather tragic. If the snowman sent any message to the world it was that life is short; soon the snowman would melt and disappear.

She also wondered if she should tell Andrew that she was pregnant. She hadn't told Nick.

By rights that should thrill Old Man Burgess.

He might not change his Will.

She'd be the principal heir, just as if Nick were still alive.

But Andrew was a suspicious old bastard. He might have the baby's DNA checked. That would be a wild thing to do. But he was capable of anything. Perhaps a simple test like the baby's blood type would reveal what had happened.

I'll have to ask Donald what type he is, she said to herself. Good Christ, he's probably something rare and exotic. If they have an exotic type of blood, she said to herself, Donald's sure to have it. He's such a fool, she added, he'll want everyone to know that he's the father. Perhaps not right now, she thought, not when Nick has been shot down and Donald was Nick's best friend.

If Old Man Andrew would only die, she thought.

*

Stephen and Jane Hopkins, still looking very rich, were wondering if they could give Christmas at Gledhill a miss.

"Do you think they'd let us leave?" Jane said.

"I doubt it."

"Of course they've got to let us leave sometime. We can't stay here forever while these yokel cops fail to solve the murder. I don't think I could stand being locked in here with you, you bastard."

"The same here. But let's talk about money. It's vulgar of course but it is something we both like."

"But is Andrew going to leave us anything? And will it be enough to keep us wishing he was dead. Or maybe helping him on his way?"

*

Parker Daniels was with Edward Burgess.

They were also talking about Andrew's money. It was the only subject anyone found to talk about.

"I like the house," Edward said. "Mimi doesn't want it. But some of those old cripples go on for ever."

That was the first time, Parker thought, that the jovial Edward, so full of Yuletide spirit, had wished his brother dead.

*

Andrew Burgess was seated by a log fire in the library. His sticks were resting on a table beside him.

Parker asked how he was.

"I can't very well kill myself. If I took a header down the stairs it might not finish me off and I'd be worse off than I am now. I wish one of them would hurry up and kill me. I suppose none of those gutless bastards have the nerve."

Andrew allowed himself a ghastly smile.

"That fat cop of yours, what's his name?"

"Sergeant Shea, David Shea."

"I've heard him talking about shooting someone. Apparently it's a dream of his. I wonder how much it would cost to get him to shoot me?"

"Now if you do get shot, Mr Burgess, I'll have to question Davy as a suspect."

"You'll have to question everyone. They're all out there plotting."

He leaned forward in his big leather chair and his eyes gleamed with malice. The eyes of a rattlesnake; an unpleasant sight.

"They want to kill me, I must get the bastards first."

Suddenly Parker wondered if Andrew had shot Nick Burgess.

Nick loved the house. That might have made him wish Andrew dead.

Had Andrew killed his nephew before Nick could get him?

It could be, Parker said to himself.

Now he had to look at the murder in a different light. Previously he had been asking the suspects where they were when Nick was shot. Now he must ask them if they knew where Andrew had been.

"God Almighty, Boomer," Davy said when Parker told him about this new prospect. "The old boy can hardly walk. How would he hold a handgun when he needs two hands to hold himself up on them sticks?"

"Maybe he sat down," Parker said. "There were chairs in the garden-room. Too bad he hasn't got a butler. He could have said 'Deal with him, Jeeves'."

Jee-zuzz, Davy thought, more whimsy. Boomer's not even pretending to be a policeman anymore.

*

Once again Parker went to see the members of the family.

It was a difficult question to ask.

Mimi Burgess knew right off what Parker was driving at.

"I wouldn't put it past him, I've seen that look come into his eyes when he was looking at Nick."

Parker didn't know how to go about questioning the others. It seemed queer to ask about a look.

Vita didn't mind being questioned again.

"You want to know how Andrew Burgess looked. Why he looked just the same as he always did."

"I mean, did he glare at anyone?"

"He always glares at everyone."

"Not particularly at Nick Burgess?"

"What the hell is this, do you think he shot Nick? Who put you up to that idea?"

Parker thought it would amaze her if he said Andrew Burgess did.

"Whenever I see Andrew glaring at us I think he'd like to kill us all," Vita said.

Margot was next. Her boyfriend, Bill Summers, had arrived from East Cheshire but she didn't seem too happy about it.

She echoed her sister's opinion of Andrew.

"Where did you go to school?" Davy asked her.

"What do you want to find out, if they teach Murder 101 there? I was at Andover and then I went to Bryn Mawr."

"High class." He made it sound as if it were a crime.

Stephen and Jane Hopkins came in. They weren't too pleased about having to see cops again.

Jane Hopkins said as much.

"But remember this," Stephen said, "while we're here we're eating and drinking free."

"Screwing for free too I suppose," Jane said.

*

While Parker and Davy were worrying about the way things had turned over, Margot was delivering bad news to Bill Summers.

"You'd better get rid of those daydreams of living in a penthouse on Park Avenue. I'm broke. Stony broke. I wonder why 'stony'? How much do you make teaching those young swine at Cheshire Academy?"

Bill told her. "I get embarrassed telling people how little I earn," he said.

"Jeepers, can we live on that? Where will we live in East Cheshire?"

Summers was thinking he wouldn't be around for long. He was planning to go back to East Cheshire alone and remain that way.

I'll kiss her goodbye as soon as I can, he said to himself. Unless Old Man Burgess decides to die right away.

*

Donald Billings hadn't been in North Holford when Nick was murdered so Parker hadn't questioned him.

Now he thought he might as well see what Billings was like.

"You were Nick Burgess's best friend," Parker said. "Did he have any enemies?"

"There was me for one."

"You?"

"I love Mimi. I have ever since I was Nick's best man at their wedding."

"Jeez, Boomer," Davy said, "everyone is putting themselves forward as a suspect."

"Did Nick Burgess know this?" Parker asked.

"I don't think anyone did."

"What about your wife?" Davy said.

"Ex-wife," Billings said. "Neither one of my ex-wives knew. They don't live anywhere near here. One's in Florida living on my money and the other one is living off it in California."

"You got a lot of money?" Davy said.

"They still think I do but I don't." He smiled. "Thinking about the troubles they're going to have is the only pleasure I get out of being down on my uppers."

"You should be careful about picking ex-wife number three," Parker said.

"I'm a fool for love," Billings said. He gave a little laugh to show he wasn't serious.

"You had to marry them?" Davy said.

"They weren't pregnant," Billings said. "The children have been spared having a father like me."

"What children?" Davy said.

"The ones who were never born."

Davy assumed the manner of someone giving advice.

"You should have just picked them up."

"They weren't like the sort you meet in burger joints."

"Some of them from burger joints is very nice girls. And they come across free after a movie or sitting down in a restaurant having some other babe waiting on them."

"Listen," Parker said, "this sociology is mighty interesting, but there's a killer needs arresting."

"Sure thing, Boomer, but it's a good thing to get to know what sort of suspect a suspect is."

Parker turned to Billings.

"What sort of work do you do?"

"Nothing much now. I was in a bank, an investment bank."

"Now you got to get yourself a real job?" Davy said.

"I'll have to, unless Andrew Burgess drops down dead."

Parker let him go.

Jack and Ottoline Smith came in next.

Parker thought at one point Davy was going to tell Ottoline she "spoke American real good", but instead he went to work on Jack, probably because he had a button-down shirt, a tweed jacket, dark gray flannel trousers and loafers with tassels.

"What do you do?" Davy said.

"I'm in real estate," Jack said.

Davy cheered up.

"Times are bad, ain't they?"

"You said it. Prices have fallen, even in Newport. I don't know what we're going to do if Old Man Burgess doesn't peg down pretty soon."

Parker let him go.

"He looked as guilty as hell," Davy said.

"They all did," Parker said and he and Davy went down to the Puritan Maid Diner for franks and Boston baked beans.

Sadie Thompson was waiting on them and Davy said she was looking real good.

"Not many dolls can walk like that, especially carry two plates."

5

Parker's daughters were coming to see him for Christmas. At least they planned to drop in on him somewhere close to or shortly after Christmas.

They were Sue and Daisy, both attractive, who took after their father by being tall. Sue was just under six feet tall and Daisy was just above it. They looked like Russian lady tennis stars.

Parker wondered how much of a holiday spirit it was entertaining your daughters with a Yuletide murder. Sarah, Parker's ex-wife, would most likely say he had arranged it to annoy her. She had never forgiven him for allowing her to run off with another man. She disliked him as we always dislike people to whom we have done some wrong.

Parker put these thoughts away and once again considered the Gledhill murder.

"Why do they call it Gledhill?" he asked Davy.

"Old Bess Gledhill, the one a hundred years ago or more. They called it Mrs Gledhill's house and later just Gledhill."

"Why didn't I know that?"

"You were always too busy being a lawyer or studying to be one. The interesting thing about Old Bess was they say she buried a fortune in gold somewhere in the house."

"Good God, do we have to bring pirate gold into it now?"

"It's not pirate gold."

"Well, it's something like it."

They went to see Bruce Dane. He lived in a modern imitation of an 18th century colonial house. It was a perfectly all right house and Parker wondered why Dane wanted Gledhill which was no longer a good example of colonial architecture. Gledhill had been much added to. It started as a Captain's House, which meant in the War of Independence it was fortified and was the place from which the armed townsmen would fight the British Redcoats. The Redcoats never came. The Victorians added to the house. Bess Gledhill was the chief builder of extensions.

"Do you suppose," Parker said, "that Bruce Dane wants the house so he can find the buried treasure?"

"I always thought he was a bit whacky," Davy said. "Still, he makes plenty of money."

Dane had a chain of supermarkets. They weren't as large as the major ones and there weren't so many but what there were brought in enough to make Dane a multi-millionaire.

There was no possibility that he could have shot Nick Burgess, but Dane had been at Gledhill the day before. He might know something.

Parker and Davy came into the house. Dane was standing there looking like a man who spent his life walking around looking at sell-by dates. He turned his head carefully as though he was worried his hair might fall off. He put two fingers of one hand up and touched the rug, which was a startling shade of black.

"Did you see or hear anything suspicious?" Parker asked.

"Do you mean did I hear anyone say he was going to shoot Nick Burgess or see anyone playing in a suspicious manner with a revolver?"

"Listen," Davy said, "we gotta ask you these things."

"Do you still want to buy the house?" Parker said. "I mean after the murder."

"All old houses have had plenty of people die in them," Dane said.

"That's true," Davy said. "And you never find no new houses haunted by no ghosts."

"Are you the only police trying to solve this murder?"

He didn't seem to think Davy up to it and he had heard, like everyone else, that Parker was a clown.

Parker knew this and he also knew that those crimes he did solve were put down to luck. Parker put them down to luck himself.

"The only thing I can say," Dane said, "is that everyone seemed to hate Andrew Burgess and Andrew Burgess seemed to hate them back."

"And Nick Burgess?" Davy said.

"I didn't notice him. I don't think I knew which one he was."

As they were leaving Dane's house, driving down the icy snowbanked road, Davy said, "Maybe he wanted Nick dead so maybe Andrew wouldn't want to live there no more and Dane could buy it. Maybe he could have hired some guy to ice Burgess."

*

It was getting close to Christmas now. Georgie Stover had put lights up outside the police station and a miniature tree in the window.

Parker and Davy came in and Georgie said, "Your daughter came in, Boomer."

"Which one?"

"I don't know. She didn't say. She was tall."

"They're both tall."

"She wanted to know when you was coming back and I said you was up at Gledhill working on a murder. She seemed to like that idea."

"I suppose she's gone for a walk. She'll come back. Tell her to stick around or go to my house. It isn't locked."

Parker and Davy went to find Phyllis Skypeck to hear if she remembered anything suspicious at the lunch time party at Gledhill.

She had a waiting-room full of patients but she let them in.

"I told you everything I saw," she said.

"What about the body? Did you find anything unusual about the body?"

"Well, he didn't have breakfast. I thought it was odd that someone would set off to go skiing on a cold winter morning with nothing to eat."

"I wonder if that suggests anything," Parker said.

After they left Phyllis they got back into the car and Parker said, "Let's go to Gledhill and see if Donald Billings is still in love with Mimi Burgess."

"This ain't true romance," Davy said, "this is murder."

When they went into Gledhill Edward Burgess said, "You've got a visitor. In the library."

Parker went and a tall beautiful girl with short dark hair was leaning over the window seat looking at the view which took in, above the snowy fir trees, part of the big lake, twenty-six miles long, which brought North Holford many summer visitors.

Jack Smith was standing next to her.

"Here he is now," Jack said.

The girl turned and said, "Dad."

"Sue," Parker said.

Jack Smith moved across the room to give father and daughter some privacy.

"Merry Christmas," Sue said. She kissed Parker. "I see you've got a holiday homicide," she said.

"Where's Daisy?" Parker said.

"She's got a new fella and probably won't be coming. She's having a good time because Mother doesn't at all approve of him."

"And what about you?"

"I'm not looking for any more broke ass Back Bay boyfriends, besides you seem to have something rather good here."

She glanced across the room where Jack Smith was standing looking at a book.

"He comes with a wife," Parker said.

"Don't they all."

"This is also the scene of a murder and Jack Smith is a suspect."

"He told me that. Wouldn't it just drive Mother insane."

"You shouldn't make that your chief aim in life. It used to be my job and it didn't work out very well."

The library door opened and Stephen Hopkins came in.

"Sorry," he said. "I thought I'd like to read a book."

"Who's the old charmer?" Sue whispered.

"Never mind," Parker said. "He's married and they're both suspects."

"He's awfully good looking."

Parker looked at Stephen Hopkins. He hadn't really noticed what he looked like, except for his expensive clothes.

"I better take you out of here," Parker said.

They left the library and met Vita and the surprisingly red-headed Margot in the hall. Parker watched these girls examining his daughter. She was obviously thought of as competition. This was all new to him. He still thought of her as very young, practically the little girl he had been left to raise when Sarah ran off with her new man.

"Good golly, Dad, they're hard," Sue said as Vita and Margot walked out of the house.

"They're just older than you," Parker said. "They've probably had some hard knocks."

"Or given them."

"Have you really seen so much of the world?"

Sue had been at an expensive boarding school and was in her first year at Harvard. Parker didn't think she had seen much of life's dirty laundry.

While they were heading for the car Sue suddenly said, "Mr Summers."

Bill Summers stopped. Looked carefully at her and said, "Sue Daniels."

He looked at Parker. "I didn't make the connection," he said.

"Neither did I," Parker said.

This was untrue. As soon as he heard that Summers taught at Cheshire Academy he had thought of Sue. But it made no difference to the investigation.

The two were chatting about Cheshire and how Sue was finding Harvard.

Parker thought, He's probably wondering how a rube cop like me can afford to send a daughter to Harvard, which costs each year more than I make. He's also no doubt wondering how I sent her to Cheshire. Maybe, he said to himself, I should tell him she has a rich mother.

He drove Sue to his house. It was in better repair than it had been but he still didn't think he had anything worth stealing so he left it unlocked.

When he pulled up at the house a neat looking BMW stopped by him. It was Dr Phyllis Skypeck.

"Hullo Sue," she said.

"How are you doing, Dr Phyllis?" Sue said.

"Keeping busy, but nothing dramatic like your Dad. I've been here seeing Mrs Wilson. She lives across the street."

"I remember her," Sue said. "She used to let me go on the swing in her back yard. It had been her kid's but he was all grown up. Is she OK?"

"I think so, she's just old. I drop in to have a chat."

"You're a good person, Dr Phyllis," Sue said.

"Speaking of which," Phyllis said, "let's have dinner sometime. I'll spring you for it at the College Inn. You can come too, Boomer, if you're not up to your elbows in criminals."

"What about it, Dad?" Sue said.

"It's OK by me," Parker said.

Sue and Parker walked into the house and he noticed that it was dusty. He hadn't noticed it before. He only ever swept up a bit.

"Jesus," Sue suddenly said, "I forgot my suitcase."

"Where'd you leave it?"

"At the police station. I was so busy looking at that hot cop who was sitting there that I forgot it."

Parker wondered if he should start worrying about Sue.

While he was thinking about this the doorbell, which Parker thought was among the things that no longer worked, rang and Georgie Stover was standing there with Sue's suitcase.

Parker wondered if Georgie was hot. Not that Parker knew what hot was. It was a word, like cool and dude, that he never used.

"Oh, Georgie, that's really kind of you," Sue said.

Georgie left and a few minutes later Davy walked in. He said, "It's started snowing pretty heavy again, Boomer. We ought to get up to Gledhill while we can. It might get snowbound."

"What are we going to do there?" Parker said.

"Give 'em the third-degree until they break."

"How could I resist that?" Parker said.

"What about me?" Sue said.

"You stay here," Parker said. "The dog will have to be taken out."

"I'll take her out," Sue said, "but she doesn't like the cold."

"Yes, she has thin hair. Still, she must get out."

"Why don't you buy her a coat?"

"I've got a plaid one, she pulls it off."

"Plaid? It doesn't go with a black and white dog and she knows it."

Davy and Parker drove through the falling snow up the hill to the late Bess Gledhill's imitation Imperial palace.

It was still freezing cold. Inside everyone seemed dressed for the ski slopes. Even the curvy ones with the most sex appeal to display had apparently thought it better to mask the ornaments for the time being.

Mimi Burgess was draped in black but the widow's weeds didn't suit her. She also kept smiling every time her eyes met Donald Billings'.

It was a smile that made her look stupid, Parker thought.

Billings was giving her a smile back, quick like a flashing light.

Parker told himself that he didn't know very much about love and sex but he knew those flashing light smiles meant they had been at it recently and were planning to be at it again in the near future.

That's a good enough excuse for rubbing out a husband, Parker thought.

But why not use a divorce court?

Well, he told himself, Nick was the heir apparent and an ex-wife wouldn't take home as much as a widow.

Parker saw Vita and Margot next. Vita looked extra cold and calculating. She wasn't flashing any grins at men friends.

Parker told himself if she had wasted Nick it would be a good idea not to look too happy.

Jack Smith had ceased looking like the All American Boy. He looked like a salesman whom nobody was buying anything from. Parker wondered if he got any satisfaction looking in a mirror and seeing how hot he was.

Then Stephen Hopkins came across the thick carpet in a pair of handmade six hundred dollar shoes, "How's it going?" he said, sounding like a bossman asking after an employee's health.

"Do you want to confess?" Parker said. "Why don't you? It would make a nice Christmas present for everyone else."

"You're quite the card aren't you, Chief. Now that I'm flat broke you must tell me what you small change guys do for a good time."

"Sit around looking miserable," Parker said.

Jane Hopkins looked at Parker and tipped him a wink. It said she knew what a jerk her husband was.

Parker looked around for Summers, Margot's sex partner and Sue's former history teacher at Cheshire. He wasn't there. Parker went looking for him and found him on the house telephone. Summers looked as guilty as a dog who had just peed on the rug when he saw Parker.

"Let me talk to Sue when you've finished," Parker said.

Summers was a big guy, about six four with big shoulders and he looked like he was ready to use this muscle on Parker. But how much of a tough guy could a prep school teacher be? Parker thought.

"I can't talk any more," Summers said into the phone.

Then he said to Parker, "She called me. What am I supposed to do? She's majoring in history at Harvard. It's only natural she should talk to me."

"Normally I'd agree with you, but you maybe gunned down Nick Burgess and I can't have my daughter going through life as someone who was best pals with a killer."

Parker went looking for Andrew Burgess again. He found him sitting by a roaring log fire in a far away wing of the house. Despite the cheery glow old Andrew still had the eyes of an unsociable reptile.

"Are they still here?" he asked. "Why don't they go home? But then if they did they wouldn't be able to steal my food and drink."

"Are you still considering shooting one of them before he can shoot you?"

"Shoot one? I'll shoot them all."

There were several glass fronted cabinets in the room, also a large glass topped display cabinet taking up much floor space. What they had in them glittered and Parker thought that this time all that glittered was gold.

"One of my collections," Andrew said. "I'm surprised those thieving relatives of mine who've come for Christmas haven't stolen them."

"What are they?" Parker asked. "Apart from looking expensive."

"Just gold."

It seemed a good idea for a millionaire to have a hobby like this, Parker thought.

Andrew seemed less reptile and almost human talking about his hobby.

"I've got lots of gold," he said and the reptile had reappeared. "More objects made of gold. They're in a safe and the safe is hidden."

"That's good thinking," Parker said. "I wouldn't leave it just lying about."

"You mean not with a gang of crooks in the house?"

"Do you know anything about Bess Gledhill?" Parker said.

"Sure I do. She had an extensive collection. That's why I bought the house. It's hidden somewhere here. I might have to take the house apart and dig up the fields."

He laughed and Parker thought it was a hideous sound, like greed set to music.

6

The College Inn was authentic white-painted colonial until they started putting in electricity, plumbing, a restaurant, two bars (one big enough for underage college kids to get tanked in) also an elevator to upstairs bedrooms just in case a girl forgot what mama told her or remembered and didn't give a good goddamn.

Over Christmas with the college girls back home pretending to behave themselves the inn was respectable. It looked something like an expensive Christmas card. The whole town looked like that, except for the streets around Forgotten Lane and Cutprice Avenue where dingy was the Yuletide decoration again this year.

North Holford was a small town and people mostly ate at home. Some years skiers filled the College Inn and the Lake House Hotel, but that was later, after Christmas.

Parker and Sue were sitting at a table in the dining-room looking just as lost as the people at the other tables.

"A nice murder might cheer things up," Sue said.

"Don't tempt fate. Maybe you should have stayed with your mother."

"No thanks, Pop, I'd rather be here with you among the walking dead." She glanced about the room. "Do you know any of these zombies?"

"I know all of them. They're not coming over here to wish me a Merry Christmas because they don't want to intrude on a father with a daughter he hardly ever sees."

"That makes me feel awful."

"You'll get over it."

"Hi," Phyllis Skypeck said.

She was coming towards their table and she was like a breath of sweet scented fresh air. Her dark curly hair was wild, it looked like someone had spent an hour, or maybe only forty-five minutes, arranging it. Like Ottoline Smith she didn't wear make up, unlike the others. Some were so covered in it they'd be like crawling into bed with an undertaker's prize corpse.

She said, "I've been up all night over at Old Compton delivering twins. They were early, came on unexpected. A boy and a girl. I suggested they call them Mary and Joseph, but she decided to name one after me and one after the father when she can remember whoever he may be. Whatever, let's get started I haven't had a thing to eat since lunchtime yesterday and that was only a grilled cheese sandwich."

The talk stopped and there was an uncomfortable silence which demonstrated that Parker and Phyllis didn't have much to say to one another anymore.

Sue was wondering what she could say to break the silent warfare. Bob Blanchard, who owned the College Inn, came to them. Before he could speak both Parker's and Phyllis's cell phones went off.

"It's a murder at Gledhill," Phyllis said.

"That's right," Parker said.

"Good Christ," Phyllis said. "I hope they've got something to eat up there."

"Who's dead?" Sue said.

"What everyone's been wishing for," Parker said. "Andrew Burgess has been found dead with a knife in his back."

"I'm coming with you. I'm not sitting here alone with the festive zombies."

"How are you with the dead?" Phyllis said.

"I don't know, I've only ever seen the dead drunk."

"Come along and we'll pretend you're a nurse. Is that OK, Parker?"

"It'll have to do for now. Later on we can go to the Puritan Maid Diner for some Yuletide grilled cheese sandwiches."

They drove up to Gledhill. Parker in the lead and Phyllis's car behind him.

*

The Christmas visitors at Gledhill were standing about telling each other that they were somewhere else at whatever time Andrew was killed. Edward Burgess showed them the body in the room where Andrew had kept his collection of doubloons, ancient coins and rare gold ornaments. Davy Shea was already there.

The cabinets and display cases were heavy duty. The glass probably couldn't be easily broken. It didn't have to be. They were all unlocked. There was no sign of them being forced.

Someone had used the key and the key was in the dead man's hand.

"It looks like he was showing the collection to someone," Phyllis said.

"And whoever it was suddenly decided to nail him to the floor?" Parker said.

There was a knife in Andrew's back. It was a big knife with a fancy handle that looked like gold. The blade was long. The sort of knife they used to tack bodies to the library floor in old time murder mysteries. This knife didn't quite do the job, but Andrew was dead as a doornail or any other fixture.

One of the windows was open. Snow was blowing in.

"It looks like the killer went out the window," Edward said.

"Or it was made to look that way," Parker said.

"You suppose any of them doubloons got curses on them?" Davy said. "I've heard about that stuff."

"This knife," Parker said, "it came out of that display cabinet. That's its twin in there."

Andrew was laid out on a three thousand dollar Persian carpet with the two sticks that he used to keep him upright on the floor alongside him.

Phyllis, kneeling down beside him, said, "Maybe I should have broadcast this before. It would have saved someone a lot of trouble. Andrew Burgess didn't have long to live. I was seeing him about it."

"It would also have saved him from a pain in the back," Davy said. "Could a lady have done that?"

"A lady would never do this sort of thing," Phyllis said, "unless she were Lady MacBeth. But the knife didn't kill him. There's no blood. He was stabbed after he died."

"I don't know what we can do about the open window," Parker said. "With this snow there'll be no footprints. We better search the house."

He glanced at Davy and wasn't too assured by what he saw.

"We'll have to get some of those college kids who play cops for us patrolling the lake in the summer," Parker said. "I'll call Georgie Stover and see if he can get anyone." He looked around again. "Where's my daughter? She can help us."

"I'm here, Dad."

She'd been standing in the doorway, trying to look like she weren't there.

"What about you, doctor?" Parker said.

"I suppose I can spare some time to look for gold doubloons. It sounds like something out of Nancy Drew."

The suspects were in the library. The log fire had burnt down and it was cold again.

"Turn the Goddamn central heating on," Summers said. "Now that the old bastard is dead at least we can do that."

"Was that the motive for murder?" Donald Billings said.

Mimi started to laugh but thought better of it and only smiled. It was a beautiful smile though, it lit up her eyes, making people see how beautiful she was. She'd practiced that smile.

Margot saw this and didn't like it, neither did her sister, Vita. They considered themselves extremely good-looking, but Mimi was beautiful.

A little later Georgie Stover came to the house. He had found someone to man the police station and he came to help the search. There were two college kids with him. Neither of them looked very sober.

Parker thought, If we don't watch out the State Police will be taking over. Maybe they should, he added.

Nothing was found.

"I'm going into the kitchen to eat something," Phyllis said.

"I'm coming with you," Sue said.

They knew Doris, the cook, and the girls who helped Doris.

Phyllis started eating. She said, "I don't feel right eating while the host is lying dead on the floor." Then she said, "But I'm still hungry."

Parker was trying to get the body removed to the hospital in Holford.

The search had revealed the safe. It was in Andrew's bedroom hidden behind an oil painting of a fierce looking woman in a white fox stole and a wide brimmed green hat. It was signed with the date 1920. The woman in the painting was the dead man's mother. The safe wasn't locked and if it had had anything in it there wasn't anything now.

"It always looked like an inside job," Davy said, "and now it's looking even more so. But where's the gold?"

"Buried?" Phyllis said.

"We'll have to hope the snow will melt," Parker said.

He started questioning the relatives again.

Stephen and Jane Hopkins were still angry with each other and they took it out on everyone else.

"Say," Davy said, "how come none of you people got no kid?"

"We got kid," Jane said imitating Davy. He didn't notice.

"Where's kid at?" he said.

"In Switzerland," Stephen said. "For some reason she didn't want to spend Christmas here."

"Gee," Jane said, "I wonder why that should be? Of course, if the old bastard didn't leave us anything in his Will she won't be going to Switzerland to have winter sex anymore."

Davy thought that didn't seem like a nice thing for a mother to say.

"She won't be going to Sarah Lawrence anymore either," Stephen said. "She can haul her ass down to the Community College."

"God, I'd like to see that," Jane said. "She's the most spoiled brat anybody has ever seen." She paused and then she said, "She's got the worst part of Stephen and the worst part of me."

"That was only natural," Stephen said, "we don't have any good parts. At least not anymore."

"Where the hell's that Will?" Jane said. "There must be at least a copy of it around here."

"Yeah," Davy said, "we shook up the place real good but we didn't find no Will. Of course we was looking for doubloons."

"And you didn't find no doubloons," Jane said, again imitating Davy. Once again he didn't get it.

The Will wasn't hard to find. It was in the top drawer of the big desk in the library. Parker called them all back to the library to let them know.

"Jee-zuzz," Davy said, "this has been here for anyone to see."

"That's what I've been thinking," Parker said.

The heirs looked exceedingly anxious.

"Go on and tell them, Boomer, you was a lawyer you can do that lawyer speak."

It was as everyone thought, Mimi and Nick got the biggest share. And Edward got the house.

"I knew I was getting the house," Edward said to Mimi. "I knew how you were afraid Nick was going to get it and you'd have to live here."

"Good God, Uncle Edward, why didn't you tell me?" Mimi said.

Her eyes weren't lit up now and the somber look made her beautiful in a different way. Vita and Margot saw this and they didn't like it, especially when it came with money.

"I wanted to tell you," Edward said, "but Andrew didn't want me to."

Stephen and Jane Hopkins didn't get a thing. Jack and Ottoline Smith and Vita and Margot weren't even mentioned.

"Well," Summers said, "I'm out of here."

"You bastard," Margot said. "And I was prepared to go to East Cheshire with you and live on your minor ducats income. I loved you."

"Love ain't all it's cracked up to be," Big Bad Bill Summers said.

"Hey," Davy said, "this is only a copy of some Will that was left round. Maybe the late old boy's lawyer has got a different Will."

"He looked the type of old bastard who'd keep writing new Wills," Vita said.

"Who was his lawyer?" Billings asked.

Edward said, "Whitney, Balanchine and Bowles in New York."

"Call them up," Billings said.

Parker, Sue and Davy were leaving. "Don't none of youse get yourselves murdered until we get back," Davy said.

"Youse can bet on it, " Jane said.

7

The prospect of it being a White Christmas was over. The temperature went up, the snow began to melt and it was helped by heavy rain. It rained all day and then it continued raining all night. Lanes that had been snowbound were now flooded. Cars had trouble and got stuck in the deep water. No one drowned but there were near misses.

Up at Gledhill they were all still drawing breath when the New York lawyer came across with the news that there wasn't any money.

Money was what the relatives had come for and it had vanished. They couldn't see why they should stay for the funeral. Old Andrew had cheated them.

"Can we get the hell out of here?" Stephen asked Parker.

"I'm afraid you'll have to wait a day or so."

"That long?"

"Well, we know where you live so we could –"

"Track you down," Davy said.

He thought Parker was being too kind to these people. He would have suspected Parker of crawling to them because they were the high class former rich but he had seen Parker being that way with the poor, with everyone.

Parker said, "It would be nice if you would remain here."

"Jee-zuzz, nice!" Davy said under his breath. It was like an aside in the theatre and it was heard by all.

Parker spoke to Summers and Summers was the only one who got angry.

"I must get back to school," he said. "I've got to get away from Margot. She keeps looking at me with murder in her eyes. You know what redheads are like, if I stay you might have another corpse on your hands."

Falling out of love with a woman in one day seemed too quick to Parker. But maybe not when she suddenly had no money.

"We've got to see Bruce Dane," he said to Davy.

"Could he have got down here and worked his way into the house with nobody seeing him?" Davy asked. "Also put the dagger in the dead guy's back, grab the loot and haul ass through the window? He don't look that fit to me."

"Maybe he's been training," Parker said. "Or maybe he knows of some collector of gold objects who's been sniffing around Burgess's collection."

They drove down Memory Hill to North Holford with the lane flowing like a mountain stream.

There was also a dip in Peekaboo Lane before the drive to Dane's colonial replica and Davy stopped the car, wondering if he could make it through.

Davy said, "Remember the last time we had flooding like this and that Wilson kid was waving drivers through and then watching them get stuck?"

As they were sailing over the flood Parker saw Moll in the back seat gazing out at all this water, wondering what new game Parker had in store for her.

Moll came into the house and jumped at the blonde standing there. Moll knew her and she knew Moll. It was Rosie the waitress. She let Moll into the restaurant when Parker took Moll out to eat with him.

Bruce Dane didn't seem surprised to see them. He led them into the room where there was a Christmas tree. There was something new about his rug today. It seemed to be on backwards as though he had slapped it on in a hurry when he saw them coming to his front door.

Rosie was a blonde with dark roots, also with what could be called an ample figure. This was on display.

She gave Davy a roguish look.

"How are you doing, Rosie?" Davy said.

"How are you doing yourself?" She touched her hair with two fingers of one hand. It was another playful gesture. "I'm back at Sam's Spaghetti House if you wanna know. I left Lobo's Rathskeller."

"I don't like spending Christmas alone," Dane said, explaining Rosie.

He was dressed in a gray cashmere sweater that cost more than Parker's suit, with an extra pair of pants thrown in.

Ditto Dane's trousers and glossy black almost patent leather loafers. It was casual but very expensive. There was, Parker thought, perhaps something symbolic about the bright yellow corduroys Dane wore. They were the color of gold.

He wondered why Dane hadn't bought himself a good wig.

He told Dane about the theft and fake murder at Gledhill.

"I got a call this morning," Dane said, "from someone who asked if I wanted to sell some of my collection. When I told him I didn't, he wanted to know if I was looking for objects he could sell me. When I asked him what he had to sell he described a few things that sounded like what I'd seen at Gledhill."

"For instance?" Davy said. He had ceased studying Rosie's charms.

"There was a gold bracelet that seemed like one Burgess had. And a necklace."

"Any doubloons?" Davy said. He liked the idea of doubloons.

"Yes, doubloons too."

"Like what the old man had?"

"I couldn't say. They are all much the same."

"What the hell is a doubloon?" Rosie suddenly asked.

"A Spanish gold coin," Dane said.

"It sounds awful romantic," Rosie said, "don't it?"

"Who was this guy?" Davy said.

"He didn't say."

"Where was he calling from?" Parker said.

"He said Concord."

"Outside Boston?"

"That's what I gathered."

"It could have been Concord, New Hampshire that's near here," Parker said.

"I didn't think of that."

"Sure," Davy said. "He could have knocked over Burgess's house and took it on the lam to Concord, New Hampshire."

"How's a lamb come into it?" Rosie asked.

"Not a lamb," Davy said, "to take it on the lam. To run away from the police. And stop interrupting a police investigation."

"OK, big shot, dot the i, wait until you next come into Sam's and see the service you ain't gonna get."

Rosie walked away from them, with a brave attempt at a slinky walk for a woman shaped like Rosie was.

"I tried to find out where he was calling from," Dane said, "but they couldn't trace it."

Dane looked annoyed, like a man who was used to getting what he wanted.

He stepped about the room, looking it over as though he were examining shelves in one of his supermarkets.

Parker was trying to imagine him getting into Gledhill unseen, finding Andrew Burgess dead on the floor and stabbing him in the back, scooping up the gold ornaments and coins and getting out of there.

But why stab Old Man Burgess? Parker wondered. The dagger was stuck in his back to make it look like someone had killed him and that someone looked like Dane. The fake murder and the open window pointed at Dane who was a collector.

They drove back to the station.

A college kid named Bob Vanderland was there pleased with himself about making an arrest.

"Good going," Davy said. "What did you get him for?"

"He was drunk," Vanderland said. "I haven't written him up yet. Do I charge him with merry making?"

"That's in some other state," Parker said. "Here a man is either drunk or dead drunk."

"You can usually get him for resisting arrest as well," Davy said. "Being drunk he will probably be confused."

"Who is it?" Parker said.

"Tim Moynihan," Vanderland said.

"Shoeless Moynihan? That's Rosie's brother," Davy said. "We better let him go if I ever want to get into her pants again."

Parker said, "It's a good thing Hapless Jones isn't listening to the way we do things here."

Jones was the man who covered North Holford for the *Holford Evening Transcript*.

"Let Shoeless out," Davy told Vanderland. He didn't like Vanderland. He was a rich kid.

Parker went home. He was surprised to see Phyllis there with Sue. Birds of a feather, he thought.

"Who's Bob Vanderland?" Sue said.

Good God, Parker said to himself, is she going to tell me he's hot too.

"He plays at being a policeman for me. Usually only in the summer. His folks have a summer house here. It's odd having him for Christmas. I suppose he's got a girl."

Phyllis left and Parker started to wonder what he could so with his daughter.

"Listen," he said, "why don't you come out with me for a drink."

"But you hardly drink at all and I'm not old enough to."

"Well, we can watch other people drink."

"How could I resist such an offer?"

They took Parker's old DeSoto.

"I tell my friends about this car and they don't believe me."

"I'm glad to hear I am a source of entertainment."

"Oh, you are. They think I'm making you up."

"Do they? Why would anyone want to make me up?"

"Their fathers are boring."

"I always thought I was boring."

"Two murders at Christmas, is that boring?"

"Only one murder. The other was a fake."

"I wonder how mother could ever have left this place?" Sue said, "Let's go to Codere's Dine & Dance, they say that's a lot of fun."

"It's the dead of winter, nobody will be there."

"Isn't that what you like?"

"I suppose it is."

He drove through the low rent part of North Holford. It was where he was from but it took many years, not until he was fourteen or fifteen that he learned how poor he was, and then it didn't make much difference. Later on when he finally did get among the rich they didn't seem to mind all that much. They thought of him as an amiable leper.

They drove into Codere's parking area and there was one low slung convertible. It was painted the sort of metallic neon blue that hurt the eyes.

When they got inside Vanderland was sitting in a booth. Then the person in the booth with Vanderland leaned forward and Parker could see red hair.

This was a big surprise.

It was Margot Cuncliffe.

"Don't let on we see them," Parker said.

"You're surprised seeing that Cuncliffe sister out with him?"

"I am."

"I'm not. She looked the type."

"But how do they know each other?"

"Uptown lowlife like them are made for each other."

Parker and Sue didn't stay long. They got into the old DeSoto and drove to Sam's Spaghetti House for what passed for an Italian dinner.

*

Later that night Parker said to himself that it was time to get proactive. He had to do some thinking.

"The trouble is," he said to Davy, "there's an abundance of suspects."

"I said that from the start."

He didn't tell Davy about Vanderland and Margot. If Vanderland was a suspect now it was better that Davy didn't know about it. Davy might let it slip.

Sticking that ornamental dagger into old man Burgess's back wasn't Vanderland's style, Parker thought.

They drove up Memory Hill to Gledhill.

The snowman on the front lawn was melting in earnest now. Green grass was showing through the snow in many places.

Parker looked up at the mountain and wondered how the eagles that were being raised there were doing. He'd like to see them.

He had to make do with sparrows. They were hiding out in the upper reaches of Gledhill. They sounded cold and wet.

He got out of the car and a big robin redbreast hopped towards him. He practically jumped onto Parker's foot.

Are they brave or just stupid? he wondered.

8

Margot was there looking guilty. But of what? She said, "I saw you and your kid out at that shack of a place by the lake. I was there with one of your part-time coppers."

"I saw you."

"I thought you did. Since Bill Summers bailed on me I've been in need of a good screw and I thought the boy Vanderland might provide it."

She watched Parker to see if he was shocked. He was still shocked but now he no longer showed it.

"You must be plenty unhappy about the Will," he said.

"You said it, Shamus."

"So you were forced to steal the gold."

"What do I know about gold except it's nice to look at. And how was I going to carry it? It must have been heavy."

She'd have been in it with someone else, Parker thought. Maybe this other one stood outside and she dropped it out of the window to him. That someone might have been Vanderland.

He went to talk with the widow Mimi. She had pulled herself together; at least she was chewing gum.

She was the merry widow now that she and Donald Billings didn't have to hide behind her husband's back.

She and Billings were sitting side by side on a sofa in front of a television set. They were talking about the price of gold.

She said, "We were wondering what the stuff stolen from Uncle Andrew would fetch if it were melted down. I don't see how they could sell the necklaces and bracelets. They'd be too well known."

A weather report came on the TV and Mimi told Billings and Parker to keep quiet. Parker thought this interest in the weather was odd. Then he thought that perhaps she wanted to go skiing or ice skating. But she was from Texas. Still, she was a sporty looking beauty and would drive men mad with desire and women mad with envy on the slopes or the ice.

On the TV the weather girl, in a dress that looked like it had been made out of the kitchen curtains, didn't seem to know what it was going to do.

Davy came into the room. He enjoyed looking at the movie star, especially after he had seen so much of her uncovered in the DVD she played for them.

"You making a new picture soon?" he asked.

"I've been sent some scripts but with one corpse after another I haven't had time to read them."

Parker and Davy continued their search. Once again they went through the house of many rooms and hiding places.

They looked out of an upstairs window and saw the movie star and her boyfriend trying to repair the snowman.

Parker went back to the treasure hunt.

"It's here somewhere," he said. "It never left the house. I'm sure no one was going to go hoofing it through three feet of snow with several arm loads of precious objects."

"But where is it hidden?"

"He was a clever old man. Too clever for us," Parker said.

Davy went off searching in one direction and Parker went off in another.

He wasn't hopeful. Walking along the upstairs hallway he saw a door partly open and a light still on in the room. When he got closer he heard voices. A man's and a woman's and both sounded familiar. He stopped by the door and listened. They weren't talking about murder, or gold. They were talking about drugs.

Vanderland had cocaine and he had given some to Margot. Now she wanted more.

She was offering him ways she could pay with no money changing hands.

"This isn't some dime bag of marijuana," Vanderland said. "This is high class coke. It costs money."

Parker wasn't armed. He knew Vanderland had at least one gun on him, probably two or three. Still, he pushed open the door. It was something to see.

Margot was sitting on a sofa in nothing but her underpants and they weren't too substantial being composed mostly of a green lace fog.

Parker thought Vanderland was pretty stupid for a college boy to be selling coke in a house that was being searched by the police.

The trouble was Vanderland pulled a gun.

Parker had just enough time to kick the gun out of Vanderland's hand and sock him. A right hook that only glanced off the kid's jaw.

Vanderland went down but only on one knee. Parker reached down and picked up the gun. He was going to tell him not to make a move but Vanderland was out of the door and running down the hallway.

"Don't touch that coke," Parker said to Margot, "it's evidence."

She just stood there coked up to her backteeth and didn't seem to understand a word.

"Come on," Parker said and grabbed her and pulled her out into the hallway clad still only in transparent green.

He could see Vanderland about to turn a corner at the end of the hallway. Vanderland looked back and pulled a gun out from around one ankle and fired a shot. Parker felt it pass close to his head. He had felt the wind from a speeding bullet before. It wasn't the sort of hobby he'd care to go in for.

He dragged Margot by one arm to the top of the stairs by the Christmas tree wondering where he could park her. Davy was standing by the head of the stairs looking more confused than usual.

"What the hell's going on, Boomer?"

"Vanderland's gone insane."

"He had a gun in his hand and he pointed it at me."

"In my case he pulled the trigger."

He shoved Margot towards Davy. "Here, get some clothes on her and then help me get Vanderland."

Davy was thinking of asking Parker a few more questions. Among them was how Margot's clothes had gone missing. But Parker wasn't there anymore.

Vanderland was downstairs running across the great hallway and then out of the front door. He still had a gun in his hand.

Turning quickly he took another shot at Parker. It sped by just over Parker's head and lodged in yet another oil painting of the Burgess brothers' mother, this time with no hat and no fox stole. She was wearing a lightweight green linen summer dress and a bullet hole in her forehead.

Parker followed Vanderland out of the door and watched him running past the beautiful Mimi and the broken snowman. Vanderland didn't run to where his car was parked. Instead, he ran towards the mountain.

Good God, Parker said to himself, I'm going to have to call out a State Police helicopter to spot him.

He set off after Vanderland. Parker hadn't stopped to put his coat on and he felt cold. Then after about fifty yards or so running up hill where the snow hadn't melted he was sweating and felt good about forgetting the coat.

Vanderland was out of sight and then Parker saw him hiding behind a good sized oak tree. He was watching Parker and he had his gun still out.

Parker thought it might be time to try talking. He stood out in the open alongside a silver birch tree which was beautiful but slim and wouldn't offer much protection even if he could get behind it quick enough.

"Bob," he said, "what do you think you're doing? A drug charge is only a drug charge and this will be your first offense. But shooting at me is something else."

He waited for Vanderland to respond. Nothing came.

"I'll tell you what, Bob, I won't charge you with trying to shoot me if you'll give up now."

Again there was no word from Vanderland.

Parker said, "You've got your whole life ahead of you. You're a rich, good-looking guy. Think of the girls you'll miss if you don't put that gun down."

"I'm not in college anymore," Vanderland shouted. "I got tossed out and then my father tossed me out."

So that was the reason why he was in North Holford this Christmas, Parker said to himself.

"Your father will get over it."

"You don't know that bastard."

"I'm going to walk up to you." He could see Vanderland quite clearly, holding the gun pointed at him.

"I don't trust you, Parker. Get the hell out of here."

"I can't do that, Bob," Parker said.

He moved slowly towards Vanderland.

Parker had put away the gun he had taken from Vanderland, it was tucked in his belt.

Vanderland stepped out from behind the oak tree.

He held his gun in one hand down by his side like a cowboy gun-slinger in a Western.

He's play acting, Parker thought.

Then Vanderland fired.

Parker didn't know where he was hit. He only knew he had been hit.

And then he knew nothing.

9

There was a swirling black pool somewhere in his head. He was dropping down into a strange place. Then he heard a voice. It was familiar but he didn't know who it belonged to. He opened his eyes and there was the face of a woman leaning down over him.

Parker knew that he knew her but he couldn't recall her name.

"Your poor head," she said. She was holding his hand.

Parker thought how beautiful she was.

"Where am I?"

"In the hospital in Holford. I thought we were going to lose you coming over the Notch."

Parker remembered having seen a photograph of this beautiful woman. In fact she looked like a photograph. Not real.

"It was the first bullet that almost did it," she said, "luckily it just grazed the side of your head."

Suddenly Parker could think clearly again. Also speak.

"There was more than one bullet?"

"That big moron hit you twice."

"Where was the second one?"

"In the right leg. He hit you on the left side of your head and in the right leg. In the thigh. It almost missed you but the bullet was still inside. We had to get it out."

"Thanks," Parker said.

"It probably hasn't started hurting yet but it will hurt. You'll be in bed for a week and then you'll have to use a cane for a few weeks more."

Parker raised his left arm and felt the bandage around his head.

"Yes," Phyllis said, "you've been in the wars and you look it."

"I'm not staying in bed."

He started to get up. He managed to get his left foot on the floor but couldn't pull his right leg out of bed.

When he did he was dizzy. He thought he was going to fall. He sat suddenly on the bed.

"I'm getting out of here in an hour or so," he said. "I've got a murder and a big gold theft to solve. Also I suppose I'll have to do something about Bob Vanderland."

"Maybe you could get about in a wheelchair," Phyllis said. She knew Parker wasn't going to do what he was told.

Then she said, "Your daughter was sitting up by your bed all day and night. I sent her home."

"What day is it now?"

"It's getting on to noon on Christmas Eve. You've been out for three days. I'll call Sue and let her know. Davy Shea is here. I'll let him in."

Davy came in. He looked troubled.

"I went after Vanderland," he said.

"Did you get him?"

"Why didn't you shoot him, Boomer?"

"I thought it wouldn't be very nice."

"Goddammit, Boomer, he was standing right in front of you. I saw it. You could have plugged him easy. I tried to get him but he kept moving."

"Where is he now?"

"There was a report of him being seen in Great Barrington, Vermonth."

"How'd he get there?"

"He stopped a car on the Notch."

"What about the driver?"

"We found the driver sitting by the side of the road in a snowbank."

"Who was he?"

"Nobody, just a guy from Springfield, Massachusetts who said he used to sell clocks and watches but the kids kept breaking in and stealing them. That is stealing some and smashing up the rest."

"What was he doing here?"

"He's Dave Wilson's cousin. He'll be staying with Wilson over Christmas. I feel sorry for him. All this and having to put up with the Wilson kid."

"I'm getting myself out of here this afternoon. Come yourself or send Georgie Stover. I'll be in a wheelchair or at least limping for a while."

"Dr Phyllis is letting you go?"

"No, I'm letting myself go."

It hurt a bit when Parker talked. That was the head wound. At lunchtime it hurt even more when he chewed.

Sue was there again, looking very tall standing beside Parker's bed. She was still there when Parker had another visitor.

This was a surprise.

He came barging into the room pushing Sue and a nurse aside.

It was Earl P. Vanderland, yet another multi-millionaire. "What have you done to my son?"

"What did your son do to my dad?"

"Who's your dad?"

"He's right here. Where your son put him when he shot him twice."

"Oh, but what's Bob supposed to do being chased up a mountain by an armed man?"

"He's supposed to stop."

Earl P. looked at Sue. He failed to see how Parker Daniels had produced such a fancy daughter.

"I understand my son is somewhere in Vermont. I suppose the skiing is better there than here."

Sue laughed.

"What's so funny?"

"Don't you know anything? Your son has been selling cocaine. He came near to killing a policeman and he stole a car at gunpoint."

"I'm not saying anything about that until I call a lawyer. I'll get a team of lawyers. There's a good one I understand in Boston, Shoester, Smith and Shoester."

Sue smiled again. "One of those Shoesters is my grandfather," she said. "My dad's father-in-law."

Earl P. looked like he was going to fall down.

"What the hell goes on here? Are you people up to something?"

The nurse who Earl P. had pushed aside came in with Phyllis who said, "I think you'd better leave, Mr Vanderland."

"Sez who?"

"Sez me."

"And who the hell are you?"

"Dr Phyllis Skypeck."

Earl P. was bored with shouting at these people and decided he might go and find other people to shout at.

*

Young Georgie Stover came into the hospital in the afternoon to collect Parker.

Take him wherever he wants to go," Phyllis said. "If he collapses call me."

"What's Davy doing?" Parker asked, "Is he trying to locate Vanderland?"

"He missed his chance there," Georgie said.

"What do you mean?"

"I came up the mountain and I saw Davy. Vanderland was just standing there. I thought Davy was going to plug him. It was his big chance to shoot someone. He's always talking about it."

"What happened?"

"Nothing. Except Vanderland ran away and then nobody could have hit him among those trees."

It had stopped raining and was getting colder again.

"It looks like snow," Georgie said. "A White Christmas."

"Maybe that'll bring the Yuletide spirit back to the folks up at Gledhill," Parker said. Then he said, "Take me up there, Georgie, I've got asking to do."

"Dr Phyllis said I should take you home."

"Whoever listens to their doctor? They get paid not to be listened to."

When they went into the drive at Gledhill the snowman still looked in need of a face lift. Parker had trouble walking. The cane didn't help much.

When they entered the front hall Edward was there talking to Jack and Ottoline Smith.

"Merry Christmas Mr Daniels," Edward said. "I didn't think we'd see you for a long time."

He looked concerned about Parker falling down.

Parker was also concerned about it.

"Take this," Edward said.

He leaned over a collection of walking sticks that were standing in something that looked like an elephant's foot. Parker hadn't noticed this disgusting object before. He didn't like it at all. But he took the stick.

"I've been learning how to walk again," Parker said to Edward and Jack, "what have you been doing?"

"Jack wants to sell this house for me," Edward said.

"You'll have a lot of buyers with it full of hidden gold," Parker said.

"I don't know if I believe that," Edward said. "After all, no one has seen Andrew's complete collection for years."

Parker said,"There was that dagger, and its twin. Also a number of objects left in the case. When was the last time you saw the complete collection?"

"I have never seen it, only been told about it. He put it in that room, but he hardly ever allowed anyone in the room."

"I wish I'd been told about that before," Parker said.

"Does it make a difference?" Jack asked.

"It might," Parker said.

Jack went upstairs and Ottoline went outside for a walk. She looked very English in a big red sweater, an old mixed heather tweed skirt and a much used pair of full-brogue walking shoes.

"I wasn't always a jolly old soul," Edward suddenly said. "I was young and miserable. Do you know what that's like?" He didn't wait for an answer. "Maybe you don't," he said. "Sure there was money, but I went to a boarding school and when I was home for Christmas my father was all the time telling me how much I cost him. He didn't say anything to Andrew. Maybe he saw the same look in Andrew's eyes that he saw in his own. They were kindred spirits. It was the same when I got into college. He never stopped talking about how much that cost him. I didn't dare go out with the boys. I never took a girl out. They cost money."

He stopped. Parker wondered if he was working up a motive for sticking a dagger in Andrew's back.

"Mother was the same," Edward said.

Parker went limping on two sticks through the downstairs rooms. He wanted to get upstairs but Georgie had gone back to the station and Parker didn't want to attempt the stairs on his own. Then he heard Sue coming through the hall calling his name. He answered her and she came running towards him.

"Phyllis told me you had left the hospital and Georgie told me you were here. What do you think you're doing?"

"Thinking about going up those stairs."

"Don't."

"Give me a hand."

Sue put one arm around his waist and helped him up the stairs. There were two dozen steps to an elegant sweeping curve and then there were a dozen more. It took time. Parker kept having to pause to take deep breaths.

"I suppose you can get down these stairs sitting down and taking them one at a time," Sue said.

Parker felt that going down the stairs was something in the far distant future. He was having so much trouble mounting the stairs that he could think of little else.

The pain in his leg which Phyllis told him to expect was there now. He had to keep himself from crying out.

It would feel good if he started to use some obscene words, but he couldn't with his daughter there.

"You shouldn't be doing this," he said.

"Neither should you."

They went into the first room they came to and there was something else Sue shouldn't have been doing. That was looking at the dead man on the floor.

*

It was Donald Billings, Mimi's true love, with a hole in his neck.

There was plenty of blood. It was all over Billings' shoulder and dripped down on the Turkey carpet on the floor.

It was also dripping down Mimi who was standing in a corner looking like an actress, preparing to scream.

"I found him here," she said. "I've been holding him. The blood was something awful."

She didn't sound real and she didn't look it either. Parker wondered why this was. Then he thought it was because she was too good-looking to be covered in blood.

"Who killed him?" he said. Then he looked into another corner and there was another Turkey carpet. There was also another body on it, a dead body with an ice pick in its neck.

It was Jack Smith.

He had been downstairs talking about real estate in Rhode Island and he had gone upstairs to check out the Gledhill real estate.

Parker had to sit down.

"Sue," he said, "call the station and then try to find Phyllis."

Sue went out to make the call in the hallway.

Parker said to Mimi, "You better sit down. Try not to look at the bodies. You can go to another room if you want. But I'll have to get a statement from you."

"I'll stay," she said.

She sat down and looked at the blood on her hands.

Sue stepped back into the room. "I've called them. Both the station and Phyllis. They're coming right away. Then we can go home. It's Christmas Day tomorrow."

"I can't go home, I'm the police chief."

"Only about one half of one now."

"I'm better off than these two."

"Can you two shut up. The way you're talking I can't hear myself weep," Mimi said. But she didn't look like she was going to cry. Far from it. There was a scary look of triumph playing around on her face.

10

The Press were all over the place like an unsightly rash. There was the story about the movie star's husband being murdered. Then there was the death of the mill owner. The reporters started filling the College Inn and the Lakeshire Hotel. Parker being shot was a sidebar. Until they learned that the man who shot him was the son of Earl P. Vanderland.

And now something new and extraordinary happened.

Two bodies in one room and the almost famous movie star covered in blood.

"Who's in charge of this?" said Johnny Peru of the *New York Daily Jolt,* wearing yellow socks and matching necktie and display handkerchief.

"The guy leaning on two canes," said Vince Vanilla, who was dressed so casually it looked like his clothes were going to fall asleep. He was from the *Boston Evening Lightning.*

There were two or three dozen other letter press and TV men and women.

Blondie Barrack was one of the TV blondies. She cornered Parker. He stood there looking hopeless with his bandaged head and sticks.

"How is the investigation going?" she asked.

Parker was stumped for an answer and looked it.

Then Sue was mistaken for a detective and was interviewed and it looked feeble when it was found out she was only Parker's daughter.

Davy came close to saving the day for the North Holford police. He didn't know anything but he looked like a cop. Sounded like one too.

The County's forensic team were there. They discovered that the blood on Donald Billings' body was the same as the blood on Mimi. There was also Jack Smith's blood on her. Thinking he still might have been alive, she said she had taken hold of Jack. There were no finger prints on the ice pick.

Davy thought an ice pick was an old-fashioned sort of weapon. Then he found there were three of them in the kitchen. There should have been four but it was stuck in Jack Smith's neck.

"It's an inside job," Davy said.

"I guess so," Parker said.

This was the sort of vague remark he kept making. It didn't go down well. The Press started wondering why the State Police weren't being called in. The Mayor of North Holford was beginning to think the same.

"What about it, Boomer?" he said. "Can you do it?"

"I suppose I might do it."

Jeeze, the Mayor thought, am I going to get in trouble having Boomer on the job?

He had appointed Parker when the North Holford police were found to be light-fingered. Two of them had pocketed some jewellery while investigating a break in at a jewellery store.

"I might call in someone from the State Police to give you a hand," Mayor Snow said.

"It would be better if he gave me a leg," Parker said.

The State Police Captain who came was a tall redheaded woman called Inez Bodegus, who had spent happy years admiring herself in uniform, especially the broad-brimmed hat and the jodhpurs. She'd never really caught anyone, which included Bob Vanderland heading for Vermont.

Johnny Peru, Vince Vanilla and Blondie Barrack didn't think much of her. They thought the lame Parker had more human interest. They liked the nickname Boomer very much. It was colorful but they thought it must be ironic. Parker didn't boom.

The story played out across the country. Big time Christmas murders in a quaint New England one-horse location.

The fathers of Jack Smith and Donald Billings came to North Holford. Everyone had been expecting more money but they were ordinary and even looked poor. It made a change up at Gledhill.

Their sons had outdone them.

"Of course," Pop Doug Billings said, "Ma and me didn't like it that he got married and divorced so many times but he got a scholarship to a fine college and then made something of himself in business."

Pop Doug worked for the bus company in the second biggest city in some Midwestern state. People kept forgetting what state it was. He might have been an actual bus driver. Something to do with buses anyway.

Harvey Smith, Jack's father, was also something not important in a small town.

Captain Inez thought they were getting in the way. She said, "This is a murder scene," as if they didn't know.

Parker was busy puzzling over the crimes. He told himself it should have been easy. Three murders and one natural death made to look like murder. All in the same house and all of the suspects related in some way. But what was the reason for the murders?

There was the missing gold. Cocaine also came into it.

Margot Cuncliffe used it. Vanderland sold it to her. Bill Summers, with only his history teacher's pay, might want to get his hands on the gold, if there was gold.

Davy then added to the confusion.

"You know, Boomer," he said, "maybe we got a crazy maniac killer guy out on the rampage."

One of the family?"

"Why not? Jack Smith and Donald Billings with the ice-pick and old man Burgess with the fancy cutlery in his back, that's the work of a loony if I ever saw one."

"But you've never seen one."

"I seen plenty."

"Where?"

"On TV and in movies."

Nevertheless Parker thought Davy might be onto something. There wasn't a logical pattern to any of it. Old Andrew Burgess was the obvious target and he had died of a heart attack. The dagger in his back was trimmings for a big second act curtain.

Once Andrew was dead there didn't seem to be a motive for the last two. They looked like the frenzied attack of someone who was not all there.

Parker inching along on his sticks found that the stick he had been given in the hospital was too short.

"May I take another of your sticks?" he asked Edward Burgess.

"Take them all."

"I only need one."

"Take them and try them out."

Edward, having got over his unhappy past, had the festive spirit again.

There were two dozen sticks. Edward got Tom and Dick, the yardmen, to take them out to Parker's DeSoto which Sue was driving.

Meanwhile the Press was active.

Blondie Barrack made a good living out of letting men slide over her. They included male bosses and men who were worth a news story. Her eyes were now on Parker.

She pitched her curves at him but they didn't work.

Johnny Peru and Vince Vanilla knew the way she worked and didn't consider it fair. They were pleased to see Parker batting her curves away into left field.

Sue saw Blondie at work and feared for her father. She said, "Watch out, Pop, that TV bimbo is out to get you."

She drove Parker home. He wasn't saying much, but he was thinking a pretty heavy bunch of thoughts about bloodstained Mimi of the Movies. Maybe she was maniac enough?

11

There was a first edition of *To Have and Have Not* by Ernest Hemingway on the table. The book case contained first editions or early editions of F. Scott Fitzgerald, John Dos Passos and John O'Hara.

Parker was thinking of reading O'Hara's *Appointment in Sumarra* again. It was a second edition in good shape. Not much flyspecking and the dust wrapper in good condition.

There was something crazy about having a book and not reading it. But when he read these books he always felt he was shortening their lives. They might wear out.

Some books he read so many times he had to get new ones.

There were many paperbacks. T.S. Eliot, Robert Frost and Wallace Stevens were among them. His choice of books was reflected in the books on sale at the bookstore he owned with Phyllis and the crime novelist, Savannah Moon.

Books were his hobby. Books and, of course, crime.

He had no desire to put the crimes on display. "I can't see myself feeling comfortable with the late murderers' shoes and socks nailed to the walls," he once told Dr Phyllis.

The door bell rang or gave an impression of a ring. It was followed by a knocking on the door.

Parker managed to get to the door and succeeded in opening it leaning on only one cane. He thought he might put a sign on the door saying "Walk In".

The bright red hair and exotic jodhpurs of Captain Inez Bodegus were on display. Behind her was a State Trooper with three stripes on his arm but with no fancy legwear.

"This is Sergeant O'Brien," Captain Inez said.

They walked right into the house and then into the living-room as if they were escorting Parker. He had an idea they might handcuff him. If they did, they'd have to carry him.

"Don't ask no questions. We ask the questions," O'Brien said.

He was like Davy Shea, Parker thought.

"Captain Bodegus," Parker said, "haven't you told your sidekick that I'm the Chief of Police."

Before Inez could answer O'Brien said, "It's not much of force you got in a one jailhouse location like this."

O'Brien gazed around the room.

"You read books?" he said.

"When I'm not entertaining the State Police."

O'Brien looked like he was going to hit him for being a wise guy.

"Where'd you get these books?" O'Brien said. "Do they come from the library at the Burgess house?"

"No," Parker said, "the books they've got there are special leather bound 18th century editions. And one wall is only leather spines nailed to the wall."

"What do you mean?" O'Brien said. Then he said, "Forget it, I don't want to know."

Captain Inez said, "We've come about those sticks you took from the corner of the front hall."

"Edward Burgess gave them to me," Parker said.

"Well," O'Brien said, "he wants them back."

This seemed unlikely. Edward Burgess had insisted Parker take them. Of course he was old and forgetful.

Parker said, "Edward Burgess told you to get them back?"

"As good as," Captain Inez said.

She was nervous, sitting on the edge of a chair with her fingers moving about as if they wanted to be holding a cigarette.

Parker thought maybe she didn't like being here.

She said, "Someone called on Edward Burgess's behalf."

"Who?"

"They didn't give a name."

"A male or female?"

"Phil," she said to O'Brien, "you took the call. Was it a man or a woman?"

"I dunno," O'Brien said. "Sometimes it's hard to tell." He gave Captain Inez a look as though he wasn't sure about her gender. Then he smiled. He liked what he saw and there was a lot of it.

"I'll call," Parker said.

"Hey," O'Brien said, "what are you trying to pull? The person who called made it sound like you lifted the things. I understand there's cops in North Holford who are known for being light fingered at crime scenes."

"That was before my time," Parker said.

"Oh yeah?"

"Oh yeah."

Parker got up and started for the house phone.

"Should you be doing that?" Captain Inez said. "You're a cripple."

"Not a cripple," Parker said, "just another walking wounded."

"A joke," O'Brien said, "I don't like the way he's always making jokes – I don't want no jokes."

Parker gave him one of those looks that O'Brien should have been wearing a bullet-proof vest to take.

"Watch out, Phil," the redheaded captain said, "he might deck you."

Parker called Gledhill, got Edward Burgess and told him what was happening.

"It's news to me," Edward said. "I never told anyone to get them back. I certainly wouldn't have had the State Police brought in."

"Here, you talk to her," Parker said.

"Her?"

"The captain in the State Police is a lady called Inez Bodegus."

"I'm no lady," Captain Inez said.

She took the phone from Parker.

"What's up?" she said.

When she finished talking to Edward she said, "Come on, Phil, let's haul ass out of here."

"Listen," O'Brien said, "how do we know if that wasn't one of Daniels' confederates and not Old Man Burgess?"

"Forget it, Phil," the captain said. "It was some kind of joke pulled on us."

Parker wondered how much of a joke it was. When the big redheaded policewoman and her sidekick left, Parker sat reading the *Holford Evening Transcript* and thinking about his visitors.

Why would anyone go to so much trouble?

He managed to get to the pile of walking sticks.

Most of them were too elaborate for a country copper to hobble on.

Then he remembered that he had a stand. It was collecting dust in the closet in the hallway. When he found it he had to roll it along. Kicking it to get it into the living-room. There weren't any simple tasks anymore.

How long is this going on? he asked himself.

He was getting hungry but he didn't see how he could make himself anything. Sue was out in the DeSoto. She was shopping.

When this tall good-looking daughter of his walked in she was carrying a pizza.

"How do you like this?" she said. "I live in Boston which is one of the great cities for restaurants and I've bought pizza. Later on we can go out for a couple of burgers."

Parker didn't tell her about his recent guests. But she had seen them.

"I saw the State Police car," Sue said, "with that big lady cop in it. What were they doing here?"

"Just trying to be police. They weren't very good at it."

The house telephone rang. Sue said, "Keep yourself seated. I'll get it." She picked up the phone.

"It's Daisy," she said to Parker. "Merry Christmas and Happy New Year," she said to Daisy, "What do you think of our murders?"

She listened for a second and then said to Parker.

"She's jealous of our murders. People in Boston who shouldn't be are walking around still breathing."

Parker spoke to Daisy and then Sarah got on the phone.

As Parker expected Sarah blamed him for having people murdered while Sue was there. He did it just to annoy her.

"I'd send her back," Parker said, "but she won't be sent."

After that, Sue did something to the television set and it worked again. They were watching *It's a Wonderful Life* when Phyllis strolled in.

"Let's see that head of yours." She took the bandage off.

"This is remarkable. I don't think you need anything on this. Now let's see you walk."

Parker let her see.

"Now without the sticks."

He almost fell.

"Try it with only one stick. You don't want to get dependant on them. There," she said when Parker walked across the living-room and back with only one stick, "I knew you could do it. How is it?"

"Difficult."

Parker started thinking about going back to Gledhill and limping through the crime scene.

He let Sue drive him.

*

The snowman was looking like he might fall down dead and the sparrows were still up in the eaves complaining about the cold.

The front door was open so they walked in.

Ottoline Smith was there dressed to go out for another walk.

She was looking at the empty elephant's foot.

"I'm going up the mountain," she said. "At least part of the way. Do you think that's cold hearted of me?" She didn't wait for an answer. "I could sit upstairs and weep, but Mimi is doing enough weeping for both of us."

"Where do you live?" Sue said hearing the accent.

"In London and in Devon in a village called Much-Bubbling-on-the-Moors. We don't take ourselves too seriously with a name like that. I live now in Rhode Island, in Providence."

"I know Providence," Sue said. "I know a boy at Brown."

"We have a house right in the middle of Brown. I suppose I should pick up a few college boys and attempt to screw myself back to happiness."

Good Christ, Parker said to himself, these girls, what were they like?

Ottoline went outdoors, across the lawn and onto the path that led up the mountain.

"Devon," Sue said, "I know an English boy who comes from there."

"Is there anywhere where you don't know a boy?"

"It's all part of a liberal education."

"I'm a guy with a two dollar education, thank God; also a night school law degree," Parker said. "If I put myself up for sale it would be in a dime store."

Vita came down the stairs. She wore a heavy sweater and looked like she might also be going for a walk. She went to the elephant's foot.

"I'm going nuts in here," she said to Parker. "Oh, screw it," she said. "I'll stay in and watch *It's a Wonderful Life*. Do you suppose I can get some popcorn? I'll see what the cook can do.'

She went off.

Edward Burgess walked in and said, "I heard voices. How are you feeling, Chief? Your head isn't bandaged and you're down to one stick." He smiled at Parker. "The mystery of the sticks," Edward said. "Everyone has noticed they're not here, but no one has said they called the State Police. What an extraordinary thing to do."

Just then Stephen and Jane Hopkins came in from a walk.

"How healthy everyone is," Edward said.

"It's more healthy now that they've moved the corpses out," Jane said.

"When can we, who are still among the living, move ourselves out of here?" Stephen asked Parker.

"Pretty soon," Parker said.

"Where are we supposed to go?" Jane said to her husband. "You said we were living free here. Not paying a thing."

"But I want to get out of this snow."

"Yeah, into the sunshine somewhere with that cheerleader."

"What cheerleader? I don't know any cheerleaders."

"Well, she looks like one. Except maybe she doesn't look intelligent enough."

"I don't know what you're talking about."

"I've seen the cheerleader. And I didn't need Philo Vance, Sam Spade or Philip Marlowe to track her down."

"Listen," Stephen said to Parker, "if I wind up dead you'll know who did it."

"I wouldn't waste my time killing you," Jane said.

"You're doing it by degrees," Stephen said.

Then they wandered off together.

"Going to see *It's a Wonderful Life*," Sue said.

Big Bad Bill Summers, the amorous prep school teacher, came in next.

He looked tough. Parker bet he'd give 'em hell if they forgot what year the War of 1812 was played in.

In Summer's right hand he held a gun. It wasn't pointed at anyone. It was a small black automatic and he held it in the palm of his hand.

"Look what I've found," he said. "You'll never guess where."

"In the snowman," Parker said.

"How'd you know?"

"There was something about that snowman that looked suspicious," Parker said.

He took the automatic from Summers and very carefully put it in his pocket.

"Are things starting to unravel," Parker said, "or are they getting more mysterious?"

He didn't expect an answer.

12

Parker examined the automatic. It was a .32 with a magazine that held eight shots. Two of them were missing.

The forensic crew from County were coming to get it.

"Nick Burgess was killed with a .32," Parker said.

"I'm getting a .45," Davy said, "That packs a wallop, but a .357 Magnum will blast your head right off."

"Anyway," Parker said, "we'll find out if Nick was killed with this gun."

"It's certain that he was," Davy said.

"You think she shot him?"

"Who else would want him dead?"

"Well, maybe a wife might possibly want a husband alive."

"Where you been living, Boomer? All the latest broads want to shoot their husband. Or re-decorate them with a knife."

"We'll be looking for fingerprints on the automatic," Parker said.

We best start fingerprinting here. Boy, are they going to hate that."

What they didn't like was the ink on their fingers. Otherwise they found it interesting.

Ottoline Smith had been fingerprinted before.

"For my Green Card," she said.

"We'll do it again, sister," Davy said.

Then he started speculating.

"If that automatic was a long time in that snowman the barrel might have got rusty and then they won't know if no bullet that killed no guy came from it or not."

Captain Inez and Sergeant O'Brien came in.

O'Brien and Davy looked like two pawnbrokers eyeing each other to see what the other might be worth.

The forensic team arrived and it was commanded by Sammie Service, a short fat man in white overalls and white rubber gloves.

He didn't actually dust the gun. A female assistant in every day clothes and no gloves, rubber or otherwise, dusted it.

This assistant was a bit taller than her boss and not fat at all. She wore a pair of large glasses that made her look scientific.

The forensic crew turned out to be movie fans. They came near to asking Mimi for her autograph.

Her prints weren't on the gun.

However, there were prints. But whose? The suspects who had been printed – Vita, Margot, the Hopkins, Summers, Ottoline Smith and Edward – were in the clear.

"Who the hell do they belong to?" Davy said.

"Try Nick Burgess's prints," Parker said.

They matched.

"Jee-zuzz," Davy said. "Are we gonna find them guys with the ice pick was a suicide pact?"

The forensic team went to view the body at Holford Hospital.

They came back looking important.

Sammie, the fat man, said, "He fired that automatic himself. The prints are authentic and his hand's got the residue gun powder on it."

"Why would Nick Burgess kill himself?" Captain Inez said.

"The guy who was the best man at his wedding was getting into his wife's pants," Davy said. "Ain't that right, Boomer?"

"It seems so."

"Love," Davy said, "what would us cops do without it?"

Johnny Peru and Vince Vanilla didn't like suicide. Peru and Vanilla wanted the glamorous Mimi to have pulled the trigger.

"Killing himself for love is OK," Peru said.

"Sure," Vanilla said, "but it ain't like a looker on trial and maybe riding the lightening."

"Do they got the chair here?" Peru said.

"It would be much the best thing to fry a dame like that."

"Yeah, it's got human interest."

Today Parker had his dog Moll in the back of the DeSoto and he took her out for a walk. Since he got shot he had to pay someone to do it, the Wilson kid among them. But today limping on one cane he felt strong enough to handle Moll. He also wanted to feed her.

Edward Burgess, an animal lover, insisted on bringing Moll into the house.

"I'll see if we've got a bowl," he said.

He came back with a number of bowls.

When Moll ate she shoved the bowl across the floor so Parker picked a heavy one. It didn't move at all.

Parker and Edward watched Moll eating. She didn't take long. It was fun to watch. It took their thoughts off murder.

But there was something strange about the bowl.

Parker noticed it first. Edward bent down and picked it up. It was very heavy. It was solid gold.

"I found it on the floor in that little room off the library," Edward said. "The room with the ivy and virginia creeper coming through the wall."

"I didn't know there was a room off the library."

"Follow me." He was pleased showing Parker something new.

Parker and Moll went with him to the library.

"Watch this," Edward said.

He was standing by the wall that was composed of fake books with only the spines showing.

He pushed something and a door opened with a sound like it was going to be followed by dust and another corpse.

There were chests in the room. Steamer trunks they used to be called.

The first one they opened was full of books, first editions that had fallen into disrepair. The second one was empty but the third and fourth were full of golden ornaments, gold doubloons, and gold bars, which were extremely heavy and worth a fortune.

"That's where the money went," Parker said.

"But producing a gold dog bowl?"

"He had a sense of humor."

"He didn't laugh much."

"But it would have amused him thinking of his heirs stumbling over a gold dog's bowl. Maybe there's more like it in other rooms."

He went to find Tom and Dick, the yardmen.

They were in the kitchen enjoying the fact that their boss was dead. One of them had one foot up on the table and the other had both. They weren't the same jolly fellows who had appeared with the Christmas tree.

They were both tall and skinny. The lack of weight was deceptive. They were strong. They were built along the same lines as Parker. He didn't notice this. He had little idea of what he looked like.

He was surprised to find that Tom and Dick weren't brothers.

One was Tom Slocum and the other was Dick Gatz. They weren't even cousins.

Slocum came from a village a few miles away called Sandbury and Gatz was from Cicero, outside Chicago. He had been arrested for robbery out West. He came East to put some distance between himself and his reputation.

Parker had looked all the suspects up. It was interesting. Jane Hopkins had been done three times for shoplifting. Vita Cuncliffe had taken her clothes off and jumped in a public fountain in Rome. Her sister, Margot, had been arrested carrying drugs. Jack Smith had a record number of parking tickets and had assaulted a policeman. Donald Billings had been charged for unlawful carnal knowledge of a fifteen year old. He beat that rap. There was nothing on Ottoline Smith, Bill Summers, Stephen Hopkins or Edward Burgess.

None of that was helping Parker find out about the gold.

"Do you remember carrying anything particularly heavy into the house?" he asked Slocum and Gatz.

"I dunno," Slocum said.

"Me too," Gatz said, "I also don't remember, and you can get them two stiffs Shea and O'Brien to work me over and I ain't remembering no different."

"If they are good boys," Parker said, "I might give you to them for Christmas."

"What ya mean?" Gatz said. "What kind of crazy talk is that? You got a lawyer, Tom?" he asked Slocum. "Maybe we should ought to get a lawyer."

"What are you talking lawyers?" Slocum said. "I ain't the one who done stick ups in Cicero, outside Chicago."

"That's because there ain't nothing worth stealing in the rube resort you come from," Gatz said.

"Can you knock that off," Parker said. "I was asking about carrying something heavy into the house."

"We told you," Slocum said, "there was nothing like that."

"Except the gold," Gatz said.

"Of course," Slocum said, "naturally the gold was heavy."

"Why didn't you mention this before?" Parker said.

"I thought you knew gold was heavy and you were asking about something else. Something that shouldn't have been heavy but was."

"Like a dog's bowl?"

"I never had no dogs," Gatz said. "I don't know what they have for dinner."

"I had a couple of dogs when I was a kid in Sandbury but they kept trying to chew up things, sometimes people, so when Spike went I wasn't allowed to get no more."

"That's sad," Parker said.

"Yeah," Slocum said, "But he also tried to give me a chew."

They weren't very good about details. Gold had gone out, in the form of coins and ornaments. It went into a truck. They couldn't agree on what color the truck was.

They didn't know where the truck went to.

When Parker left them he was walking without the stick. He put it in the elephant's foot. His leg was stiff but he was going to be a long distance man again soon.

It also meant Sue wasn't going to be manhandling the old Desoto. He could put Sue somewhere safe while he went after the bad guys.

He didn't tell the State Police about the gold and he didn't tell Davy on account of letting Davy know would be like making a radio broadcast or putting it on the front page of the *Holford Evening Transcript*.

O'Brien, however, suspected something was up.

"You been away a long time, pal," he said. "Feeding no dog don't take no time like that."

"Leave him alone, Phil," Captain Inez said.

"I'll leave him lying in a heap wishing he had taken up some other trade," O'Brien said.

Parker didn't think much of the State Police and O'Brien was a bad example of a bad lot.

Suddenly O'Brien took a swing at Parker. He was big in the chest and shoulders. He most likely packed a punch. Parker ducked. O'Brien was swearing.

"Phil," Captain Inez shouted. Then she shouted Phil a second time. When she shouted it a third time Phil was not able to answer.

He was laid out on the floor.

"It's true what they say," Captain Inez said, "the bigger they are the harder they fall."

She winked at Parker.

Parker said, "Keep your boy quiet. I've still got to find out why they're wearing bullets, daggers and ice picks this season."

13

For guy who wanted to sit at home reading books Parker had wacked O'Brien right out of the ballpark. He turned to the lady State Trooper and started apologizing.

"Never mind," she said. "Phil's got a thing for me but I knock him back every time he starts hitting on me."

There's romance in the air, Parker thought, and scattered corpses.

"Phil's got it in his head that I go for you." She suddenly had a roguish look and that made Parker think of running.

He stood there trying to think of a way to be missing.

Dr Phyllis came into the house.

Phyllis took in O'Brien who was sitting in a corner with a handkerchief pressed to his lower lip trying to stop the blood.

"What happened to him?" Phyllis said.

"Love," Parker said.

*

The Press were leaving. The College Inn and the Lake House Hotel were back depending on skiers.

Sue kept pestering Parker to let her in on the Gledhill murders. He didn't tell her about the gold. A seventeen year old girl couldn't be trusted with that information. Even a seventeen year old girl who got into Harvard when she was sixteen and was studying things Parker couldn't pronounce.

Parker called Boston but the former Sarah Shoester wasn't available.

"She's out somewhere being in love," Sue said, heavy on the sarcasm.

"A seventeen year old daughter shouldn't say that about her mother," Parker said.

"I can't pretend it isn't happening. She left us with you to run off with her lover."

"I've got a dim recollection of that."

He was wondering how to get Sue interested in something other than murder.

The only thing he could think of was boys. Girls were interested in them.

Where could he find a boy? One who wouldn't get her involved in something as dangerous as crime?

Phyllis might know of someone. He asked her.

"Isn't this above the call of duty?" she said.

"I've got to keep her mind off murder."

Finding someone up to Sue Daniels' level would be difficult, Phyllis thought. Sue had shot through school and got into college when she was barely sixteen. She was also loaded with money, or her mother was. All six feet of little Sue came on like seventeen going on thirty-six, but that was only something she had learned in the movies, or maybe from her mother, who had Major League round heels. At Sue's age Phyllis had done little else but study. She continued like that until she was out of medical school working in a hospital in Boston. Then she realized that she knew an amazing amount of things, but not what the rest of the girls had been picking up in the backseats of cars. She was trying to cure that loss.

Anyway, she kept a look out for something to take Sue's mind off murder.

Then Phyllis met a boy. He was so good-looking she had an idea she might grab him for herself. But he was only twenty.

He was the nephew of a doctor in Holford. He was at Williams and he and his mother were visiting Holford over Christmas.

Phyllis thought that old milltown wasn't a festive place.

"I know he's terribly bored," the doctor uncle said. "His mother and I have old times to talk about. Brother and sister stuff. But he's well out of it."

The doctor looked at the pretty Dr Phyllis and he thought, She's older than he is but he won't mind that.

Phyllis must have known what he was thinking from the expression on his face.

"It's not for me," she said. "Of course normally I'm the sort of woman you have to keep nephews away from. But not this time."

The doctor smiled. He didn't find Phyllis funny but he knew he was supposed to.

"I'll bring him along this afternoon," he said.

Phyllis was impressed when she saw the handsome nephew. The kid was bored, she could see that.

"You ought to go to North Holford," she said. She could tell his uncle had already told him what she wanted. "There's a girl that I know. She goes to Harvard. She's visiting her father."

"I wouldn't mind meeting her," he said.

She wondered if she should tell him how tall Sue was. "I'll arrange for you to meet her at the College Inn." Then she paused, "You know," she said, "it might be nice to know your name."

"Summers," he said, "Jake Summers."

Unfortunately Phyllis didn't make the connection. When she did make it, it was too late.

14

Snow had come back in the night and was still falling.

The view for Sue looking out of the window at the College Inn was limited to twenty feet. After that there was a dense fog.

From the window she watched some birds. Their feathers were puffed up against the cold.

Why don't they fly South for the winter? she said to herself. Then she added, But why don't I?

Parker had dropped her off at the College Inn. The police station could usually be seen from the inn, but not today.

Parker getting Phyllis to find a chum for Sue was bizarre. But the police station was close enough for him to drop in and check out the chum.

All that snow outside. Just looking at it made Sue feel cold. In a civilized country a girl could get a snort of something to keep out the cold. The drinking age had dropped down to eighteen once but it was back up to twenty-one again. What must Europeans think of such a law? she asked herself.

College students had to manufacture false identification making them twenty-one. She had such a document. It couldn't be used here because people knew how old she was.

She saw Phyllis's car burst out of the fog. It was followed by a low-slung foreign sports car.

A boy who didn't look at all like a jock, a type she didn't like, got out of the two-seater and joined Phyllis. He looked like a preppy, but so, she told herself, do I.

Phyllis gripped this prep school product coming up the path. It was definitely a tight grasp. More, Sue thought, than was necessary to keep Phyllis from slipping and falling down. That was typical Dr Phyllis. Sue knew about the horny doc.

They disengaged when they came across the room to Sue. They still looked like a couple. Phyllis certainly attracted men.

Dad's smart to keep away from her, Sue said to herself.

The boy got most of Sue's attention. She wondered if she could talk about T.S. Eliot with him. Also James Joyce, Marcel Proust and Virginia Woolf.

But Phyllis had no sooner introduced them (by their first names only) when Jake started talking about the murders at Gledhill.

Bob Blanchard was waiting on them. He also wanted to talk about it.

Jake gazed out of the window.

"I had a hell of a time getting over the Notch," he said, "and it looks like I'm going to be snowed in here."

"I've got some nice rooms," Bob Blanchard said.

Phyllis said, "It also looks like I'm going to be snowbound. I better get out of here. So long, you kids, have a nice time."

Jake was certainly taking Sue in. About as much as Phyllis had been taking Jake in.

Being admired was pleasant. Sue was used to it but it was always nice when it happened again. She worried that she might have lost whatever it was that she had. In a mirror she saw the bad side of things. Other girls she knew spent much time tilting their heads around at angles that made them look good.

"What a dreadful place this is," Jake said.

"It beats Boston if you want to ski."

"I suppose so."

"What do you want to do, Jake? Shall we go for a walk?"

"In this blizzard?"

"It would be something unusual."

Jake said he'd sneak her a drink. That is if they'd serve him. He had false ID.

Sue said, "I'm worried my Dad might burst upon the scene. He works just down the street."

She was thinking it wouldn't be at all bad for Parker to act as a father figure, telling her she was doing wrong things. He wasn't actually much of a father. Maybe he was years ago but she couldn't remember much of that.

"Look, Jake, shouldn't I know your last name in case someone comes in and I have to introduce you."

"Summers."

"What?"

"Summers."

"Are you related to Bill Summers?"

"He's my uncle."

"He's also one of my Dad's murder suspects."

"What do you mean?"

"My Dad's the Chief of Police. Besides, I don't like Mr Summers. Listen, I'll be seeing you."

"You're not going to walk out on me?"

"Ski out actually."

She called out to Bob Blanchard:

"Do you have some skis I could borrow?"

"I do. Boots too. You're going skiing, you and Mr -?"

"Summers. No, I go alone."

"I'll come too," Jake said.

"No you won't."

"This is dreadful. What am I supposed to do in this berg?"

"That's your business."

"But I only came here to see you. And I like what I see. You know that. I could tell you could see it."

He stood over her watching her put on the ski boots.

Sue said, "If I hang out with you I'll meet your uncle and have to be polite to him."

"Would that be so difficult?"

"Sure it would, he's been making a terrible show of himself with his over sexed redheaded sweetheart running around naked and coked up out of her head."

"I don't believe it."

"It's true. We don't just have murders here."

She went to the front door of the inn carrying the skis, put them on and pushed herself across the snow. Going down the middle of the street looking like she was having a good time in the fog and snow.

She stopped outside the police station. Opened the door and said to Georgie Stover, "Tell Dad the date he fixed up for me is all over and never got started."

Georgie had no idea what she was talking about but he said, "OK."

She smiled at him. Then remembered how hot he was and smiled even more and said, "Thanks a million,

Georgie. If you ever get free maybe you could show me around."

"Not around Gledhill, your father wouldn't like that."

"What about a movie?"

"The only picture house now is in Holford. We'd never get over the Notch."

"Well, how about a cheeseburger? Think it over. I've got to get going. See you, Georgie."

Georgie, who had no idea that he was hot, sat there wondering if the chief's Harvard College daughter had been making fun of him.

*

Phyllis was driving very slowly but came near to hitting some lunatic who was skiing in the middle of the road.

Then she saw who it was.

She wondered what Sue Daniels was doing.

Phyllis was by the College Inn. Jake's red roadster was still there covered in snow. She parked her car by a snow drift and bent almost double, she went up the path to the front door.

Bob Blanchard was there glaring at the snow that was keeping customers away.

"What happened to the love birds?" Phyllis said, taking off her now wet coat.

"She flew away and he's having lunch."

"I'll join him."

Jake looked up, saw a girl crossing the room, thought for a moment it was Sue, then his face registered disappointment.

I'm a terrible person, Phyllis told herself. It made her feel better, as if she weren't responsible for her actions.

He wasn't all that much younger than her, only a half dozen years or so.

If I were the man and he were the girl no one would think anything of it, except how lucky I was.

He hadn't finished. She ordered lunch, trout and a Waldorf salad, and bought a bottle of wine.

"Sue has proved a wash out?" she said.

"And I really like her. I mean I really really did, the first time I saw her I did."

"You couldn't have seen anything more of her than the first time."

Young love, she thought, what a crock it was.

She ordered another bottle.

I'm plying him with drink, she thought.

"How about a brandy?"

"I dunno."

"Listen, my cars still running. Do you want to come to my place? I've got plenty of room. I got you into this and I feel guilty."

"I've got a room here."

"That's perfect. We can have the brandy upstairs."

"If you don't mind."

God, she thought, he really is simple. I ought not to do this. Then she wondered how good her underwear was. It was nothing slinky setting off the curvaceous shape of a vivacious lady. If he's twenty he won't be bothered about that.

They rode upstairs in the elevator.

"Does everyone think my uncle is a murderer?"

"Your uncle?"

"William Summers."

"Big Bad Bill?"

"Yeah."

"Good God I never made the connection."

"Do you think he is?"

"I wouldn't know. There's quite a collection of suspects. I'm just the doctor. Once I let everybody know that the gunshot and the ice pick have not been good for them my work is finished."

"Do you think I could go and see Uncle Bill?"

"I don't see why not."

"Will you take me?"

"I might."

They went into his room.

She was standing right up against him. The bed was just behind his back. She wondered if she'd have to push him down on it. Rape wasn't her style. Or maybe it was. Young Summers was exceedingly slow on the uptake.

She took one sweater off and then the other two; three basic colors. She went everywhere layered in the winter.

She started unbuttoning her blouse.

He stood there looking at her as if she were a magician about to perform a trick.

When she took it and her skirt off and was standing there in her knee length non-fun drawers she thought something must be done.

"Jay," she said.

"Jake."

"Right. Sorry. Jake, are you OK? Are you gay?"

"Gay? What do you mean gay? I'm not gay. Everyone knows that. Listen, I could tell you stories. Gay? That's a good one."

He was worked up now. He gripped her.

Twenty is really wonderful, she thought. Then when it was over she thought, What a bitch I am. And I'm also starting a hangover.

"Will you take me up there to Gledhill? I'd like to go up there. Maybe I can solve the crime. That would be something."

Jesus, she thought, he's ten years old.

"Sure thing, Sherlock," she said.

15

There was another girl who was thinking about herself. There was nothing unusual about this. Thinking about herself occupied close to ninety per cent of Mimi Burgess's time. Much of this were dark thoughts about her past.

Since she was twelve men had been gripping her.

The fault was her mother's. Her mother was a failed actress. That is she worked in a shoe shop in San Antonio and day-dreamed about being an actress. She wanted Mimi to be one. It was the old story.

Also men gripping beautiful girls was the old story. She didn't get to like it until she was fourteen. After that she enjoyed it so much she barely graduated from high school. She took some theatrical lessons from a fat old woman who claimed to have known Rita Hayworth's kid sister, then Mimi went to California where Hollywood was, and the groping was more entertaining; she got an agent; a beautiful girl was bound to. Then she got into pictures.

She made some money. Enough to finally tell her mother to go to hell. But how long am I going to last? she wondered. Will I ever make it big, really big?

She met Nick Burgess when he thought he might be a writer and had one movie script and ideas for half a dozen more.

She was called Mimi Garz then, and when she married Nick she started called herself Mimi Garz-Burgess.

She got many compliments on the hyphen. Trouble was it didn't look American, producers thought she was English.

Anyway Mimi was thinking about love. She liked being loved. Nick had loved her but she couldn't love him back. Donald Billings, she had loved him and he had loved her back but not enough. Both men were dead so she stopped thinking about them.

She wanted the whole world to love her. Well, she wasn't sure about the whole world. There were actresses whom both men and women liked. Mimi knew she wasn't one of them. Women didn't like her, on the screen or off. There was a song that went "don't you wish your girlfriend was hot like me". That could be Mimi's theme song. But she was not a success with the ladies.

To get back to business, business was business and Mimi, the widow of a man who shot himself and the lover of a guy with an ice pick in his neck, was upstairs in her room reading a script.

Her agent sent them to her. He hardly ever actually read one. He found out what it was about and then flipped through to see how many pages Mimi's character appeared on and how many lines she had to learn.

Mimi did the same thing.

She couldn't understand most of what she read. Filthy language and violence, also sex scenes with no clothes or hardly any, she knew what that was about, which was bringing the teens and twenties in. The little morons apparently couldn't get enough of that.

If there was some subtlety of plot it was a mystery to her.

Mimi put the script down and thought she might fall in love again. This meant she wanted to find a man who would fall in love with her.

She wasn't that far gone. She wouldn't be light until August. There might be big trouble making a movie when you were pregnant, but Marilyn Monroe managed it but Marilyn Monroe was in an era of big women and could get away with her belly showing. The size of that ass too. You wouldn't dare haul an ass like that around to a studio today.

Maybe she wouldn't have the brat. She was only having it because it would please the old miser. But he was dead, and dead broke.

She felt cheated. The old boy had no assets. Only gold. Hidden gold.

There wasn't anyone with money among the suspects, except maybe that guy with the comic rug, Bruce Dane, who owned a dozen supermarkets.

He was old and ugly and not that rich. He also looked too sad for a good time, a real melancholy Dane; she'd seen Mel Gibson playing that Prince guy.

She thought she might fall in love with someone just to keep in practice.

She told herself she'd do it with the first man she saw when she went downstairs and then she went downstairs and the first man she saw was that tall policeman who looked like he should be a Texas Ranger in an old-fashioned cowboy movie.

*

Parker came in stamping the snow off his shoes. They were only shoes but they were big and heavy enough to be called boots. He had an old tweed jacket that looked like it should have patches on the elbows and an old sweater that looked like he had knitted it himself.

Edward Burgess heard the sound of feet and came into the room.

Mimi was still on the stairs planning an entrance.

"If this snow keeps up," Edward said, "you'll have to stay here."

"We'll see. Maybe I can get a plow to get me out."

There was noise from the stairs.

Parker turned just in time to catch Mimi.

This is going to be easy, Mimi thought. Then she said to herself, I might even find the gold with the help of this hayseed cop.

Davy came in just as Mimi seemed to spring into Parker's arms.

"Jee-zuzz," he said. "Do you do all your own stunts?"

"The only stunt I do is when I'm pretending to get screwed."

"What a way to talk."

"But that's what you like."

"Well, yeah, but parked somewhere on a lovers' lane or standing up outside a wall in good weather."

"Thanks for sharing that with me."

Davy had left the door open.

"Come in, moron, close the goddamn door," Mimi said.

"Boomer, do I have to take this?"

"She's a grieving widow, Davy."

"I'll say she is. But I've come up to grill some more of them suspects. At least the ones who haven't been murdered yet."

Mimi said, "Why don't you try that cocaine bimbo, the Cuncliffe broad, Margot."

Davy went off in search of suspects before they got themselves killed.

"Are you finished?" Parker said to Mimi.

She was standing close to him. Pressed up to him in places.

"What? Do you want to give me the third degree?"

"I don't know what to do."

"You'd think a cop would know that. Don't you have to pass a test or something to get your job?"

"I was a friend of the Mayor's."

"Corruption is what made this country great. Shouldn't you ask me a few questions."

"I don't know what to ask yet."

"You don't know what to ask me? If I ever meet someone who wants to kill a guy I'll recommend this town."

"I suppose we do look like big time yokels in the way we don't solve murders."

"Wait until a few more bodies show up before you start bragging about how bad you are."

"Did you shoot your husband?"

"No, he did that for me."

"What about the ice pick?"

"I never use one. I like Scotch and soda, no ice. And very little soda. In fact I don't really drink much. I find I can be just as disgusting when I'm sober."

"So I'm not going to get a confession?"

"I'd like to help you out. If no one comes through give me a call and let me know what you want in the way of a confession."

"That'd be nice of you."

"You got to find something to do with snow up to your armpits outside and a gathering of prize winning bores inside."

"I feel sorry for you."

"Who wouldn't? But there is something you could do for me."

"You want to know why I'm called Boomer."

"No, I'll keep that excitement for later. What it is, I've been sent a script for a movie set in a rube location."

"In New England?"

"Maybe. I don't know. But one town full of bumpkins must be very much like any other. Could you let me in on it? Maybe show me around?"

"Davy might do it."

"That fat cop with the mouth? This ain't a burger and bra picture. It's got class. I don't get screwed until half way through and then I keep my clothes on, a tweed skirt and a twin set with pearls - it's a period piece. But tell me, why aren't you gripping me? Why don't you love me like the rest of the chumps?"

"I can't love anyone. I don't know what love is. At least that's what my ex-wife said when she was checking out of the homestead."

"What did you say to her?"

"I said, 'Thanks, that clears it up'. 'Clears what up?' she said. 'Why I can't wait for you to go', I said."

"That wasn't very nice."

"It was as nice as I could be at the time."

"But you're over her now?"

"Yeah, I sent the guy she ran off with a box of cigars and the name of a good shrink."

*

Davy found Ottoline Smith in the library by the fire. She was standing there looking like an advertisement for Taylors of Old Bond Street.

"I say," she said, being lots more stage English than she ever was at home – she almost said "my good man" but she thought that was a bit much and then she said it.

"I say, my good man, I dropped into that college tavern for a spot of luncheon and I saw the local bicycle, that doctor person, all over some young man, a new one I've never seen before."

Davy couldn't understand the way she talked.

"Dr Phyllis?"

"Yes, the one who was all over my husband."

"He was dead, she was examining him."

"I'm talking about sex. Being dead is clearly a drawback. I'm referring to that dismal lunch time party where they first met."

"Dr Phyllis is often over eager."

"I suppose I shouldn't blame my husband, but I could have killed him at the time."

Jee-zuzz, Davy said to himself, this is it, the tweedy English bitch is confessing to murdering her hubby.

"Did you kill Billings too? Or did you just find him wearing the ice pick in his neck and it give you the idea to do the same to the late Smith?"

"If I did you'd be the last person I'd tell."

Davy thought he'd find somebody else. The cokehead redhead Margot. He had seen her half naked. She might be wearing something along the same lines today.

16

Phyllis was slightly hungover and feeling just a few inches away from despair.

That kid Jay, Jack or Jake had been a mistake. Nice while it lasted but still something she thought she should have done without.

Especially when she remembered seeing that English piece, Ottoline Smith, in the College Inn. Bob Blanchard also had a big mouth. Of course they couldn't tell anyone who didn't already know her little failing.

She was going out to start her car when she got a phone call.

In the deep snow the ambulance at Holford Hospital couldn't get over the Notch to North Holford where there was a kid who had hurt himself.

She knew the kid. He was Jimmy Birchard, about twelve or thirteen. He was sick a lot of the time. A poor specimen, sick, frail and unhappy.

Still, he was said to be good in school. Brilliant. But Phyllis heard there was some trouble.

She could walk to his house. It was a shabby sort of place in Mean Street. It needed paint. Something should be done to the roof as well. There weren't any other houses like this in this street and then she remembered that Parker's house was falling down just around the corner.

Peg Birchard answered the door. She was smoking and looked worried and poor. Fred Birchard, the husband, had run away with a waitress. Phyllis wondered if other towns had waitresses like North Holford did.

Phyllis asked about the injured kid.

"He was out sliding on his sled," Peg said. "I keep telling him not to but he did."

Phyllis remembered now what the trouble was for Jimmy Birchard. His mother didn't approve of school. She wanted him at home doing errands for her.

Phyllis followed Peg Birchard up a not too clean stairway to a not too clean room where Jimmy was in bed looking frail and unhappy.

What happened?" she asked.

Peg said, "It was down that hill they call Ten Bumps. I tell him don't go but the other kids do. That Wilson kid is always egging them on."

"My head," Jimmy said, "I banged my head into a tree."

There wasn't any bleeding but he couldn't keep anything down and he kept falling asleep.

Good Lord, Phyllis said to herself, he's fractured his skull. I can't leave him here alone in all this dirt with Peg going out to work. Peg had been a waitress but since she lost her figure she was washing dishes.

"I did wrong," the kid said.

"Never mind, Jimmy, I used to go down Ten Bumps. We all did."

"I never," Peg said.

"Listen. We've got to keep his head still. He shouldn't be moved. He should be in hospital."

"How am I going to pay for the hospital? I can't pay for no hospital."

"Never mind about no hospital. I know a lady. Mrs Wilson —"

"She related to that Wilson kid?"

"I don't think so. Anyway, she's a retired nurse. She'd take Jimmy in until we can get him to the hospital."

"I can't pay."

"That won't be necessary. I'll look in a couple of times a day and Boomer Daniels' daughter, Sue, is home across the road. I'll get her to look in. I'll get my car started and come back for Jimmy."

"If you say so."

Peg stood there with the cigarette in her mouth. She was still frail and unhappy too.

Phyllis telephoned Mrs Wilson.

"I'll make it worth your while," she said, "I'll give you a hundred dollars a day."

"That's too much," Mrs Wilson said. "I won't take that much."

Phyllis got her car started and slid and skidded back to Peg Birchard's home.

Moving the kid was a major project.

"Keep your head still," Phyllis said. "Don't look down."

Christ, she thought, moving him like this I'm going to kill him. The kid read books, far advanced for his age. She wondered if she could get him some books to read. But reading might not be good for him.

Jimmy, wrapped up warm, got to Mrs Wilson's home which didn't need paint or a new roof and was as clean inside as a well run hospital. "Here we are, Nurse Wilson," Phyllis said.

Mrs Wilson laughed. "I haven't been called that for years."

They got the kid settled.

Phyllis went across the street to Parker's house.

Sue was there, trying to clean up the place. She had repaired the TV and also an ancient gramophone.

"Listen," Phyllis said, "I've just brought a kid to Mrs Wilson's across the street. Could you drop over to the house and look in on the kid? He's got a possible fractured skull and I can't get him over the Notch to the hospital in Holford."

"What can I do?"

"Keep an eye on Mrs Wilson. She's not young anymore. And you can talk about books to the kid."

"Kids' books?"

"No, he's bright. You can talk about F. Scott Fitzgerald and Ernest Hemingway."

"I don't like Ernest Hemingway."

"Well you can tell the kid why."

"Jesus, what a Christmas. But I suppose it's better than murder. What's the kid's name?"

"Birchard."

"Like President Rutherford B. Hayes? The B was for Birchard."

"Wait till you see his mother, Peg. She figures big among the kid's tragedies."

⁎

Silence stole down on Gledhill. Freezing air seemed to keep sound away.

Mimi gazed out from a high window in her bedroom. The room had a large four poster bed covered by an old-fashioned handstitched New England quilt.

Mimi, who was dressed for cold weather, got on the bed again and pulled the quilt over her.

Love was on her mind, it was never far away.

She was thinking of the past. There was a terribly rich man who said he loved her. He asked her to marry him. She said yes because there was little else to do that day.

And then something amazing happened. Really unbelievable. The Social Register was going to drop this turkey if he married her.

The Social Register? She didn't know what it was. It was something she had heard about in books, maybe Edith Wharton, that female edition of Henry James, had mentioned it. It was about high class rich people in New York in the old days.

But no. It apparently was alive and kicking this man out if he married an actress. *Forbes* magazine ran the Social Register. She'd never read *Forbes*, never even seen a copy. She only knew that each year it listed the top millionaires in America. Probably nowadays, she told herself, that would be the top billionaires.

Well, the bastard had dropped her. She didn't have a gun to shoot him with or a knife to stab him. The lucky son of a bitch, she would have gladly killed him.

No jury of real Americans would convict her. She might get three years and be released after six months.

That was a few years ago but Mimi could still get growling angry about a man preferring a register to her.

Parker was downstairs also gazing out of a window. Alongside him was Johnny Peru, the *New York Daily Jolt* reporter.

"You got any motives, Boomer? I got to milk this somehow or they'll think I've been fooling around with some trim up here on expenses. Vince Vanilla's already got a rocket from his tab."

"I'm looking for a motive'" Parker said.

"Ain't that gold enough?"

"Maybe."

"Gold is only a maybe? Speaking of trim, I seen Sergeant Davy having a good time grilling that redheaded Margot dame. This time she was going formal. She was wearing a brassiere."

"It's the festive season. Her sister Vita is a looker too, and she keeps her clothes on."

"I got to get something," Peru said again about the lack of news.

Parker felt sorry for him. He felt sorry for everyone. It was getting worse every year. He kept meeting new people to be sorry for.

"Listen," Peru said, "you got something new on that kid, Vanderland, who shot you? The college boy dope peddler, son of big shot money man Earl P. Vanderland."

"He's been arrested in Newport, Rhode Island," Parker said.

"Newport?" Peru said.

He had a phone and started calling his story in. "Newport," he said, "is a great place to get arrested for a rich kid . . . Maybe he was thinking of stealing a yacht and sailing away . . . Whose yacht? I don't know whose . . . I suppose Earl P. Vanderland's got one . . . How many feet? I dunno. If he had one it would be big . . . ocean going? . . Sure it would be ocean going. You got all that? . . . Good. Make it look like I'm working."

Peru stopped talking and looked as the big and sometimes not so bad looking Captain Inez Bodegus entered the room.

Captain Inez was an outsized Spanish beauty, but she looked depressed.

"I've been up questioning Mimi of the Movies," she said.

That, Parker thought, was why Inez was depressed. Standing alongside all that beauty wouldn't be good for the Bodegus self-esteem, even if she was armed and in jodhpurs.

"Did you get anything?"

"No, she just asked me if I ever heard of the Social Register. What is it?"

"Something where rich people have a good time reading about themselves."

"What the hell are you talking about? Sometime I think you're talking in code. Next time spit it out on the wall so I can read it."

Sergeant O'Brien came in and looked absolute harpoons at Parker.

Captain Inez saw this.

"Watch out, Phil," she said, "or Boomer might give you two bloody lips this time."

"That'll be the day," O'Brien said.

"A bloody nose then," Inez said, "and a black eye. Maybe two black eyes if Boomer's feeling generous."

"I've got to get out of here," Parker said, "before you've got me chainsawing him."

Inez smiled but she looked like a member of the chorus and not Carmen anymore.

17

Someone had to go to Rhode Island and collect Vanderland and bring him back to face charges for selling dope and shooting Parker.

"I suppose I could go," Parker said.

"Are you kidding?" Davy said. "Them R.I. cops take one look at you they'll arrest you."

"What for?"

"For dressing so bad."

Parker gazed down at his clothes. They were ageing badly, covered in premature wrinkles. The trousers were long past retirement age and the shoes were in need of emergency treatment.

"They'd think you was a phoney, come to Newport to help Vanderland escape."

Parker knew he had an image problem. When he was a lawyer he came into court once and the cops had grabbed him and put him in the dock. He won that case. The jury liked him for the laughs he gave them.

Parker wondered if Davy would do any better. Davy would have to pass through Boston and he might stop off to see a New England Patriots' football game or go to see Boston Celtic play basketball.

"We'll ask Captain Bodegus," Parker said. "It might be nice to get her out of the way. She can take

Sergeant O'Brien. That way I won't have to hit him for a few days."

*

The snow had been cleared off the roads. Things were moving in North Holford again. You could get over the Notch. Phyllis thought she better get Jimmy Bichard to the hospital in Holford. She went to Mrs Wilson's. Sue Daniels was there.

"This kid," Sue said. "He's been telling me about the *Book of the Dead*, from ancient Egypt. Have you ever heard of King Umas of the 5th dynasty? Or Queen Mentuhotep of the 13th dynasty?"

"Mentuhotep sounds like a town down South somewhere. A sort of second-rate Memphis, Tennesee," Phyllis said.

"The kid's amazing," Sue said. "I wonder what he'll be like when his head's cured?"

"So you had a good time?"

"Are you kidding? The kid's invented a new way of boring grownups. I felt like I wanted to get myself into the *Book of the Dead*."

"I think you need your own pyramid for that. Anyway an ambulance is coming for him."

*

Earl P. Vanderland also made it over the Notch.

He saw that the lake was still frozen, with skaters on it, and he thought this was rather old time and backward. The lake should be drained and something that could make a profit built on it. That was progress.

If it got flooded over that would be in the future and the men who did the building would be faraway bringing progress to some other place.

He worried about his boy Bob.

Trouble was he didn't seem able to get his boy Bob off a minor bit of dope peddling and cop shooting. And a small town Minor League cop at that, a cop who probably needed to get shot in order to earn his pay.

He strode into the North Holford police station as if he were going to repossess it.

When Bob Vanderland saw his father walking towards his cell he backed up until he was flat against the wall with an expression on his face like he was expecting to be hit.

Earl P. didn't like what he saw.

"Robert," he said, "how come you have such a narrow forehead? My own is bulging with brains. Don't you ever eat fish?"

Good heavens, Earl P. thought if I get the sap sprung out of here I'll have him next to me until his trial comes up.

"You like it here, Robert?"

"It's OK." He was worried about what Earl P. would do to him if there weren't iron bars beween them.

Earl P. went to the front office to talk to Parker and the other cops.

He said, "I understand you are thinking to charge my boy Bob with removing by death some poor people."

"Poor people, they got a right to live," Davy said.

"Do they?" Earl P. said. "I don't see why."

"They weren't exactly poor," Davy said. "They was rich once but they're broke now."

"That makes them worse," Earl P. said. "Listen," he added, "you ought to find the real killer. There must be some more poor people around here who could have done it."

"We've got suspects," Davy said.

"Now," Earl P. said, "how about if I give you a little extra pay, say ten thousand dollars, if you pick on someone else? Meanwhile keep the kid behind bars."

"We couldn't accept any money," Parker said.

"Couldn't we?" Davy said.

"OK," Earl P. said, "how about if I offer ten thousand bucks reward to whoever names someone and it leads to a conviction?"

"We can't stop you from doing that," Parker said.

"Ten thousand?" Davy said. "What's ten thousand? You can't even buy a new car with ten thousand."

Earl P. stood there, unmoving but thinking. Twenty-five or thirty thousand wasn't much to him. But he didn't like paying more than an item was worth. He couldn't see his boy Bob going for that kind of money.

He had in fact a new car. He had driven it over the Notch this morning. He had come all the way from his winter place in Sprained Ankle, Vermont in it. He didn't like it.

"I'll make the reward a new car," he said. "Practically new," he added.

"If someone comes up and proves it was your kid who did it," Davy said, "does he still win the car?"

Earl P. hadn't thought about that, but he really didn't like the car.

"Sure thing," he said.

18

Mimi the minx was still keen about keeping up with her hobby, which was making men fall in love with her. The trouble wasn't getting the men to love her. It was what you did with them afterwards. You couldn't put them in a glass case. They were the sort of collection you wanted to get rid of once the game was won. But they didn't go away. Instead they stood there gazing at her like baffled bovine.

But the game with Police Chief Parker "Boomer" Daniels was not over – it had hardly started.

She had leaped into his arms like leggy Suzanne Farrell in *Slaughter on Tenth Avenue*.

Since then, however, Parker had ignored her. He was busy talking to possible witnesses.

Sue and Phyllis were aware of Mimi's new interest in Parker. Flame-haired Margot knew as well. She saw Parker side stepping Mimi in the upstairs hallway.

He had come to ask Margot about Vanderland. Everyone had asked her about Vanderland, including this copper, many times before.

This time it wasn't about drugs. The tall cop in the hand-me-down clothes wanted to know about the ice pick murders.

"Shouldn't you ask Mimi about that? She was the one in the room with the dead men, covered in their blood. I imagine it looked like a scene from one of those rancid movies she's in."

"I've asked her."

"From what I've seen she wants you to ask her some more."

Parker ignored this. Or tried to ignore it. Davy, Georgie, Sue, Phyllis, the Hopkins, Ottoline Smith, Hapless Jones, Johnny Peru and Vince Vanilla had all enquired about his relationship with newsworthy Mimi.

Now in Margot's room, with another four-poster bed with an antique colonial New England patch-work quilt, Parker was talking murder.

He wanted to know if Margot thought Vanderland was capable of it.

"I suppose he could be," she said, "if he was bored and couldn't think of anything else to do."

She crossed her long legs, smiled and flicked her red hair away from the eye it had been covering. It was an eye she knew she could make smoulder. Her figure in a green top and skirt was looking pretty goddamn svelte this morning when she ran her eyes over it for a couple of hours in a mirror.

She thought she could make the cop sweat.

Parker simply stood there waiting for her to say something important about Vanderland.

She couldn't think of anything important to say. Vanderland wasn't at all important. It had been hard to take him seriously, even when he was pointing a gun at her demanding money.

Then she stopped trying to smoulder and said, "Maybe he did ice pick those guys. Maybe they were buying dope from him and forgot to pay. Or couldn't pay, same as me. They couldn't offer him payment in kind like me," she added, smouldering a bit around the eyes.

Parker went to see Vita, svelte in black, in a room with yet another four-poster bed with colonial New England hand-stitched patch-work quilt.

Parker ignored the long Cuncliffe legs as she crossed them.

"Look, Chief," Vita said, "I don't know why Jack Smith got himself killed. What about going for a spot of lunch at the College Inn? I could use some bright lights and sophistication after being pinned down in this mortuary with no tidings of comfort and joy."

Parker though you should never mix business and pleasure. But could Vita really have killed anyone? Could she have spent that much time away from a mirror?

"The roads have been cleared," he said. "I suppose we could make it with only a bit of skidding."

Immediately Vita wondered what it would be like eating opposite a man wearing a shirt like that shirt. What would people think? What people? A pack of hayseeds. Besides Mimi would, for some mysterious reason, be driven mental with jealousy.

*

Parker was driving his old DeSoto, a tribute to Detroit in its golden years.

Vita didn't see it that way. She kept wondering if the car would explode.

The DeSoto slid down Memory Hill from Gledhill and then over the ice to Rattler Road leading to North Holford town center.

The old village green was still under three feet of snow. The big Christmas tree in the middle of the green was frosted with snow, and just beyond it but still on the green stood the white-painted steepled colonial church, a wooden copy of a stone church in England. The settlers had wood in the New World's forests but not much stone, except the stones in their fields which broke their plows.

Parker was looking at the way the snow had drifted over the path to the front door of the College Inn and thought maybe he'd have to carry her. The high-heeled shoes she wore were suitable to be svelte in, but were no use for snow.

Parker picked her up and carried her into the inn.

She said, "I understand you caught Mimi when she took that dramatic header off the stairs. I'm lighter than she is, aren't I?"

Parker let her answer that for herself.

The Police Chief caused a stir walking into the Inn with a woman in his arms.

"Is she injured?" Bob Blanchard asked, rushing forward with an anxious look on his face.

Parker stood her upright.

In the dining-room a table of tourists who had been heading further up country than North Holford but got bogged down in the snow, looked in wonder at the glamorous woman with the tramp.

"She must employ him to carry her through the snow," one of them said.

"If he were mine I'd buy a pair of snow-shoes and leave him at home," another said.

Phyllis was also in the dining-room. She was looking for Jake Summers who was upstairs in his room wondering if he could hide under the bed if she broke in. Youth calls to youth and he was pining for Sue. The fact that she had so mysteriously walked out on him added to her allure.

Phyllis stopped thinking about the boy Summers when Parker came in.

She loved Parker after a fashion, but she couldn't see what appeal he had for the sexy Vita. Anyway, Parker shouldn't go for a woman like Vita. What he wanted was a down-home girl, like Phyllis felt she was when she woke up in the morning before she remembered the night before. That lasted about thirty seconds.

He's probably going to arrest her for murder, she said to herself.

Meanwhile what Vita was doing was trying to get Parker to arrest someone else. She was pretty liberal the way she spread the guilt around.

"Mimi is the one with a motive. First there was Nick, her husband."

"That was suicide," Parker said.

"Mimi was in love with the late Donald Billings. I saw her sneaking into his room." She was silent for a moment then she said, "That Ottoline Smith. She looks down on me. What a lot of nerve. She must know I look down on her, and I got in first. She probably did in her husband with the ice pick and Billings walked in and so she had to do him in."

"But the ice pick was in her husband's neck, which seems to show that Billings was killed first."

"Does it? I think she thought her late hubby looked better wearing an ice pick."

There was another pause. The smouldering eyes narrowed and a frown of concentration appeared.

"That Jane Hopkins," she said. "She's a real bitch, and probably went crazy."

"What would be her motive?"

"She doesn't need one. She's the type who runs amok. In an uncontrollable frenzy. I'll bet Stephen isn't her first or even her second husband. I wonder what happened to the others?"

She stopped again. Then she said, "And Bill Summers, you know all about him. There's been some nasty gossip about him. There'd have to be, with him running around with my sister."

"Could she have killed anybody?"

The question didn't upset Vita.

"She's too busy taking dope and acting like a tramp to have time for something like only murder."

Parker thought he should say something but he couldn't think of anything to say.

Vita said, "I called my mother to wish her a Merry Christmas but she didn't seem to know who I was. Speaking of drink, do you think I could get a martini, two olives and easy on the Vermouth."

She hadn't mentioned Edward Burgess, nobody ever did. Parker wondered if he should.

Later he was on Memory Hill aiming the old pride of Detroit at Gledhill when Vita did mention him. "That old boy Edward," she said. "He's got the motive. With Old Andrew dead Old Edward gets it all. Not that there was anything to get, but at the time he wouldn't know that. Anyway, Andrew was a candidate for Murder One. I took one look at those serpent eyes of his and thought how pleasant it would be to dust him down with a few pistol shots."

"I'd watch what you say," Parker said, "there may be a detective listening."

Vita took no notice. She said,"There's that boring rube with the bad rug and grocery stores. He collects gold doubloons and things. I'm sure he must be guilty of something with the type of women he goes out with."

The DeSoto sounded like it was going to give up the ghost on the steep slope up to Gledhill. Luckily Parker had chains on the tires.

"There's that Vanderland kid," Vita said. "But what about Earl P.? You could run for the Senate if you nabbed him. I don't think he'd even have to be guilty."

The DeSoto finally crept up to Gledhill's front door. Parker had to carry Vita again.

"There he is," Vita said, "Old Edward looking like Mr Brownlow about to rescue Oliver Twist."

Johnny Peru and Vince Vanilla were standing alongside Edward.

"And those two," Vita said, "they'd do anything for a story. What's a couple of dead guys to them?"

19

Parker was at the police station with Davy and Georgie, who was looking at the snow and remembering when he was in the Army in yet another hot place; he kept forgetting the names, if he ever did know them. His sweetie pie, Isabella Sargo, from Pudenda Street, told him that she had dreamed of him every night. Several times, in answer to her prayer to the Blessed Virgin, the Holy Dove had resurrected Georgie and flew him down to her. Nine months later a baby boy with lots of red hair, was delivered. A beautiful child but he possessed a remarkable likeness to Red Mullins from Corkscrew Lane.

"There's a suspect," Georgie said. He pointed to Ottoline Smith, bundled to the ears, walking on the old village green. She was kicking her way through the deep snow, gazing up at the stainless blue small town New England sky.

"What's she doing?" Davy said.

"Looking at an American sky," Parker said.

"That's goddamn eccentric," Davy said. "Why do you think that? What's she expecting to see looking at sky, there's nothing up there."

"Up above the world you fly," Parker said, "Like a tea-tray in the sky."

Jeez, Davy thought, a tea-tray in the sky. He means a saucer, a flying saucer. And it won't be long now, he thought, before North Holford will be looking for a new police chief.

Parker said, "I asked her what she was doing when her husband was killed and she said she was out looking at the sky."

"And you believed that? Why would you believe that?"

"It sounded like the truth to me. She said they've got some beautiful clouds floating in blue skies in Devon in the village of Much-Bubbling-on-the Moors where she comes from. But she said stainless blue skies reaching up to oblivion is rare, especially in the winter."

"So what do they have there?"

"Rain," Parker said.

"Jee-zuzz, Boomer, you trying to tell me that English babe didn't kill no one because she likes our blue skies?"

"That's right," Parker said.

"Why?" Davy said. Again he thought Parker was losing it. Parker was going seriously bughouse.

"Why?" Parker said. "If she were any kind of even second rate killer she would have thought up a better alibi than that."

"She didn't look too unhappy when she found out her husband was dead."

"That's the same thing," Parker said. "A homicidal wife would have worked up a few tears."

"And Old Edward?" Georgie said. "He's the last one anybody would suspect."

"I've been worrying about him," Parker said, "but then I've been worrying about all of them."

"We got Bob Vanderland locked up right here," Davy said. "Maybe we shouldn't look no further than that. He maybe didn't kill anyone but he tried to kill you. And besides, he's the sort of guy who'd look good in the State Pen. I don't like that Earl P. none either," Davy added.

"He seems to be the peoples' choice," Parker said. "Too bad he wasn't anywhere near North Holford at the time."

*

Sue Daniels was thinking of going out and looking for something hot in trousers. Her mother was a pain, especially at the festive season, but had Sue stayed with her Mother she might have found something to do in Boston.

There was a knock at the door and a shout and Phyllis walked in.

"I suppose you're bored," Phyllis said, "with nothing to do."

"How'd you guess that?"

"I've got something for you that will keep you busy."

"Do you want me to help you at Holford City Hospital? I suppose there's a multitude of broken limbs with the excess of ice this season."

"No, not exactly," Phyllis said.

"Are you talking about that Bichard brat with his unwholesome interest in King Umas of the 5th dynasty?"

"How'd you guess?"

"It's that look in your eye."

"Listen," Phyllis said, "he hasn't got a fractured skull, but Mrs Wilson's got flu. She can't have him. And you know what his mother's like."

"Do I?"

"I told you. She works all day and most of the nights washing dishes at the restaurant. The kid's got a cracked rib and a sprained ankle. He can hop around but he can't be left on his own."

"OK, but tell him to give his brain a rest."

"You should talk. I remember you and your IQ. You should have some fellow feeling for Jimmy Bichard."

"Where is he now?"

"Sitting in the car outside."

"Well, pull him out and limp him in."

Phyllis went out and then the Bichard kid appeared in the doorway looking like a delinquent version of Tiny Tim.

He hopped into the room on one of those ugly aluminum walking-sticks that hospitals provide.

He gazed around the room as if he must do something about the furniture.

"I suppose I can read those books," he said. "The hospital library wasn't up to much. I only read half of them and I felt as if I were doing something damaging to my mind."

He took a book down from the shelf.

"This ought to do for an hour or so."

He read *The Dream Life of J. Hector Possum* by P.S. Parson

> *Arise awake you silly*
> *Girlies sleeping*
> *The hippos wiggle grinning*
> *In the mud.*
> *They grin at the repitious*
> *Parrot's tautology,*
> *But do they grin at me?*

Arise awake you silly
Girlies sleeping.

Lesbians at the Ritz bar
Talk of Jake La Motta.
How good it is to sit
Drink a lotta,
And talk of shopping.

Silk Hat Harry needs
A stiff one.
Where is Silk Hat Harry? Silk Hat Harry, he
Ain't here no more, the goon.
But Broadway Willie will
Be along soon.

Arise awake you
Silly girlies sleeping.

Oh, I don't know but I bin told
Esquimaux pussy's mighty cold.

"That's the stuff to give the morons," said Jimmy, "just obscure enough to keep them baffled."

He saw the stand in the corner with the walking sticks. He hopped over, threw down the pathetic hospital cane and picked up a polished gold handled walking stick.

He said, "This has got to be Victorian. It ought to have a ruby with an oriental curse on it."

"We can only hope," said the bored and longing Sue.

Unknown to anyone else in North Holford Bruce Dane had a visitor.

Sinister Earl P. Vanderland had crept in under cover of a villain's darkness and curled up in a guest room.

Rosie from the Spaghetti House was a frequent houseguest. She had, she said, a girl pal named Cher at the Spaghetti House who wasn't very particular. Did Brucie want Rosie to fix Earl P. up with unfussy friendly Cher?

"It's not her real name of course. Her real name is different. Delilah. The same as some dame who give a guy a haircut. That seemed too old-fashioned so she changed it to Cher."

Dane, who wished Rosie would stop calling him Brucie, thought Earl P. lived on a higher level than Cher a.k.a. Delilah.

Earl P. had come to see Dane because Earl P. thought perhaps the chain of New England supermarkets could inch its way West. If Earl P. could find the parking space Dane could plant more supermarkets and ruin a lot more downtown shopping centers.

There were, of course, more anti-social things than ruining towns but Earl P. had already done most of them.

Besides he wanted to keep his eye on his idiot son locked up in a North Holford cell.

If it came to a trial Earl P. was fairly certain that he could produce his boy Bob's school reports and get him off on grounds of stupidity. DNA was another thing – maybe he could find out that the kid wasn't his. He thought he would convert to Rome and pray at the nearby gargoyle festooned church of St. John the Cousin in Holy Smoke Street if that was the case.

In the meantime Earl P. was admiring Dane's collection of gold doubloons and oriental curios.

He learned that the late Andrew had had a much bigger collection that was now mislaid at Gledhill.

I wonder, he thought, how can I get my hooks into that?

Earl P., like most lazy rich men, didn't like wasting his time and the time he spent trying to keep young Bob out of trouble was, he thought, time wasted. But if he could get his hands on the Gledhill gold, that would be worth all the time he had wasted in this backwoods locale. He thought of this and it gave him pleasure; much more pleasure than Cher could provide with her thin arms and damp kisses.

20

It was a bleak and depressing mid-afternoon, with a growing darkness.

Sue was in the house with Jimmy Bichard. Moll sat on the big old-fashion brown leather sofa alongside Jimmy.

"I think I've had enough of Ancient Egypt," Jimmy said.

Moll looked up at him, waiting for him to say something about food.

"Egypt is all objects. I think I maybe more interested in Ancient Greece. It isn't about things, it's about thought. The Philhellenes have the right idea."

Moll looked at him as if she were going to agree with him, maybe start telling him of a dandy production of *The Wasps* that she had seen.

There was the sound of a car's tire chains on the icy road. The car pulled up outside and Sue heard footsteps on the front porch.

Thank God, Sue thought, and then the never-locked front door swung open and two men walked in.

They both wore balaclavas. One of the balaclavas was black and the other was green. The green one had a gun.

One of the men grabbed the sticks while the other one pointed the gun at Sue. Jimmy launched himself from the sofa and landed on the back of the man with the sticks. The intruder went down on all fours.

Moll ran about barking at this new sport.

"Jimmy," Sue shouted, "don't be a hero."

Jimmy was trying to pull the black mask off.

The man didn't say anything but he waved an arm at the one with the gun.

Jee-zuzz, Sue thought, he's going to shoot us.

But the gunman, with his eyes a startling blue looking at her from inside the green balaclava, just stood there pointing the gun at her.

Then he fired but it went over her head hitting somewhere high on the yellowy wall where there was a varnished bookcase. Henry James got it right through the real leather binding, *Daisy Miller and Other Stories* dropped to the floor.

The gunman with green head and blue eyes turned and ran. The other one shook Jimmy off his back, picked up an armload of gold handled walking-sticks and ran out of the house.

Sue heard the car starting and then she heard the sound of broken chains.

She went outside and there was the legendary Wilson kid.

"Did you get the license plate number?" Sue said.

"No," the Wilson kid said, "but I undid their chains for them."

*

Davy and Georgie were in the station.

There was some noise outside. Davy looked out and saw a TV camera crew. Blondie Barrack was in town again; a camel hair coat which was opened with up-lifted bosoms poking through a sweater, which was blue to match her eyes. Blue mittens also reflected the dramatic blue of Blondie's gorgeous eyes, but the vapid smile of minor celebrity proclaimed stupidity.

In front of her, knocking on the door, was Mimi.

"Open up," she said, "I got page one prime time coverage here."

Davy opened the door.

"OK, fatso, where's Boomer?" said Mimi. "I've got to have him here. I'm giving the world the story of men killing themselves on account of unrequited love."

"Listen," Davy said, "I'll be a stand-in for him. It might do me a lot of good with the local quail if they see me on TV with a big time movie queen."

Then Parker pushed his way through the crowd, which now included among the press Hapless Jones, Johnny Peru and Vince Vanilla.

He was going to ask what the trouble was when the phone rang and there was real trouble.

*

Sue and Jimmy had the Wilson kid still with them when Parker and Davy arrived.

The Wilson kid had both pockets full of assorted cookies and two doughnuts that Mrs Green, the baker's wife, had given him to go away and stop frightening the customers.

The Wilson kid said, "Maybe I done something that will lead to the capture of the Gold Handle Gang." He supplied free of charge a name for the crooks.

Sue started telling Parker the story but the Wilson kid interrupted her. "With the chains undone," the

Wilson kid said, "they might skid into a snowbank and be stuck there."

Parker picked the Henry James story off the floor. The bullet had gone through it and into the yellow-painted wall. He dug it out and put it in an envelope.

"I'm going to have to leave you," he said to Sue. "Let's go," he added to Davy, "we might get lucky."

Blondie Barrack and her TV crew had followed him and were now blocking the way. Hapless, Peru, Vanilla and Mimi were also on the porch.

Parker and Davy got into the squad car. The loose tire chains left a trail to follow which they did out to the last of the houses, where the car had turned right, on Rattler Road.

The snow was different here and there was no more trail to follow. Davy said, "There's two ways he could go, Boomer. Left up Memory Hill to Gledhill or straight ahead to the Notch."

"It's certain that they're connected to Gledhill, but they don't want to trap themselves there. Head for the Notch."

It looked like the end of the world. The bare branches of the black maple trees were bending back and forth in the wind making the same spooky noise as Parker heard coming off the frozen lake. This time Ottoline wasn't around to take his mind off business.

Davy said, "There's something wrong here, Boomer, going to all that trouble for an armload of second-hand walking-sticks."

"They've got solid gold handles."

"Yeah?"

"Do you know the value of gold today?"

Davy shook his head.

"Neither do I," Parker said, "I'll have to look it up. But since business went bad gold has gone up."

"But a few gold handles?" Davy said.

They drove on and at the bottom of the steep way up to the Notch they saw a green four-door Buick. It was pushed into the side of the road under the trees.

Parker and Davy got out.

There were tracks in the snow. The footsteps of two men.

They followed them up towards the top of the mountain.

Along the way they found a walking-stick.

"I guess it was getting heavy carrying two dozen of those," Parker said.

The footsteps led them to a place where skiers started on a long straight run down the mountain.

"I never took to no skiing," Davy said. "It's a rich kids' sport."

"Not in North Holford it isn't."

"Well, it looks it."

Because so many skiers had gone down this run it was packed a hard icy gray. There were no foot-prints. They walked down, slipping and almost falling. Several times they had to hold out one hand to prop themselves up.

"What are we going to find at the bottom, Boomer?"

"Nothing, I suppose."

"Why bother?"

"There might be something."

"You're trusting to your luck again, Boomer."

"You never know."

"Hey, here's another one."

There was a walking-stick on the icy snow of the downhill run.

Davy bent over and picked it up.

"It's a nice cane," he said. "If you was a high class cripple this would be just the thing to limp along on."

They got to the bottom of the run and there was a pile of walking-sticks, most of them ebony black and all with gold handles.

Davy said, "Why go to all that trouble if they only leave them here?"

"I think they want us to carry them the rest of the way."

"Where to?"

Parker pointed towards Gledhill. The house, still looking festive with snow on its roof, was close by; in the distance, just above the trees, life in the form of cold winter sunlight was breaking through the clouds.

21

Parker went home. The crowd had got off his porch and were now in the middle of the street. Mimi was performing.

She was starting to get to be a joke. There were some people laughing as she told how men died for her. The rest were looking puzzled by this new sort of insanity.

Parker went into the house. Phyllis was there looking at Jimmy's sprained ankle.

"Was there anything familiar about them?" Parker asked Sue.

"They wore masks and it happened so fast. I looked mostly at the gun. The one with a gun was wearing a green balaclava."

"Green?"

"I think if was emerald green, or perhaps jasper."

"Jasper?"

"Jasper green. Or maybe grass green. Not olive or bottle, but it could have been seagreen."

"I'll put down vaguely green."

"That should do it. You don't want to be pedantic."

"One was young," Jimmy said, "and the other wasn't."

"What was he?"

"A grown up."

"An old grown up or a young grown up?"

"I don't know. All grown-ups look the same to me."

The boy genius turned to Captain Elmo in the Sunday newspaper funnies. Captain Elmo was a super hero who could spring over skyscrapers with a single leap. He also glowed in the dark like St. Elmo's Fire. It was the first boyish pastime that Sue and Phyllis had seen Jimmy indulge in. Parker could have told them that Davy was also a Sunday supplement fan of Elmo the Bounder.

Moll sat and watched Jimmy. She was bored. She kept jumping into Jimmy's lap disrupting Captain Elmo's adventures.

"Somebody should teach dogs to read," Jimmy said, "it would help them to escape boredom; much more than barking."

Moll heard the word dogs and remembered that it had something to do with her. She started to bark and leap about in a manner meant to please.

"Does anyone know the value of gold?" Parker said.

Sue said she could find out easily on the Internet. She had her computer with her.

"You could work it here?"

Sue knew just how much far back in the last century Parker was. He had once asked her if you had to put a stamp on an e-mail.

In no time at all Sue had the answer.

"I can't believe it," Parker said, "it's just over one thousand, six hundred and fifty-eight dollars an ounce."

"That's gone up a couple hundred since the last time I looked," Jimmy said.

He took no further notice. Captain Elmo was glowing in the dark, preparing to leap over the Empire State Building.

Parker said, as if he was talking to himself, "This is creating a mighty big motive for someone."

"But why did Andrew turn his assets into gold?" Sue said.

"That's what I've been wondering," Phyllis said.

Parker said, "The only thing I can say is that Andrew had a weird sense of humor."

Parker was thinking there could be gold running through the length of the sticks. It would make a stick very valuable.

*

A walker found a gun in the deep snow on a mountain ski trail. It matched the description of the gun fired at Sue. The walker and the gun were now at Gledhill.

Georgie Stover, once a soldier knew about guns. He went to Gledhill with Parker.

"The gun's a .44 Magnum," Georgie said.

The bullet that was fired at Sue and which Parker had dug out of the wall was from a .44 Magnum.

The walker who found the gun was new to Parker.

"She's Maud Brewster," Edward said. "The new cook."

She was tall and thin and Parker didn't think she looked like a cook.

Flame-haired Margot came out of the billiard room where she had been sniffing coke and practicing making a cannon shot.

She looked at the .44 Magnum and said, "I know that gun."

"Is it yours?" Parker said.

"It was Jack Smith's. I suppose it went to his widow."

"Ottoline Smith?"

"She's the only widow I know."

"Shall I pull her in, Boomer?"

"She's at the Lake House, Georgie."

"I'll get her, Boomer."

"You don't have to," Edward said, "she's here. But she's such a nice girl. I'm sure she's done nothing wrong."

"Has she moved from the Lake House?" Parker said.

"No, I invited her for lunch now that we've got a new cook."

He attempted a small bow to Maud Brewster, who was standing there still not looking anything like a cook. She was like a corpse looking for an undertaker.

Ottoline was in the library reading an English novel which ended with an Englishman's idea of happiness, a house near a pub and a season ticket to his favorite football team.

She was looking homesick, but she smiled when Parker came in and the smile made her look fit again for winter sports. He was carrying the gun in a see-through plastic bag.

"Oh," she said, "that's mine, or rather, Jack's. I haven't seen it for some time. Where did you find it?"

"I didn't. A woman named Maud Brewster ..."

"I know her. The new cook. She's a terrible cook. I'm glad I'm staying at the Lake House. When the chef there is sober enough to keep upright he's good enough so you don't get sick every time."

Moll was asleep in front of the library fire. She stirred in her sleep, dreaming of summertime when windows were left open. Not only in her own house but all over town. She loved leaping through an open window, especially if people were inside eating.

Ottoline wasn't taking the .44 Magnum seriously.

Parker wondered if the gunman might have been female. This is getting too complicated for me, he thought.

He had brought the walking-sticks into Gledhill. Now he decided that was a bad idea.

"I'm taking them away," he said.

"That's a good idea," Edward said. "Once those bandits have been to your house they won't come again."

Bandits was a curious use and Parker saw Edward smile at his own old-fashioned word. Parker began to wonder if Mimi was the only actor in the house.

"I'm not taking them home. I'm taking them to the station."

Edward frowned, only a slight wrinkling of the brow.

"Is that really necessary?"

"They're key pieces of evidence."

"Are they really?"

"Someone was willing to pull a gun and fire at my daughter trying to get them."

"How did you ever manage to follow them?"

"The chains on their snow tires had been undone, it left a trail."

"That was stupid of them not to put the chains on properly."

"You'll have to forgive them. Somebody undid the chains."

"Who was that?"

"The Wilson kid. He doesn't seem to have a first name."

Parker called Moll. She managed to lift herself from the fire and come to him.

Parker and Georgie gathered up the walking-sticks.

Maud Brewster, still un-cooklike, stood silently watching.

The gold knobs were something to see.

"Do you have a safe at the station?" Edward asked.

"We do, but nobody has remembered the combination since two thousand and two. I'll lock them up in a cell."

"Is young Vanderland still there?"

"I'm afraid so."

When Parker and Georgie got back to the station Davy was eating a cheeseburger.

"How's Vanderland?" Parker asked.

"I give him a cheeseburger same as me. He don't appreciate it though. How's that Margot redhead doing? Keeping her garments on?"

"She was practicing billiard shots."

"Billiards, that's a rich guy's game. Why can't she shoot a couple of frames of pool instead?"

"They don't have a pool table."

"Yeah, rich guys. Say, what's caviar, some kind of rich guy's fancy chow?"

"It's fish eggs."

"Jee-zuzz, the things rich guys will eat. They'd be much better off giving their money away and eating poor."

"Why do you ask about caviar?"

"Bob Vanderland wasn't grateful when I give him the cheeseburger. He said he could eat caviar anytime he wanted. He said when he was in France he ate plenty truffles too. What's truffles when it ain't candy?"

"You aren't going to like this, Davy. They're fungus dug up by pigs in France. They're pretty strong smelling."

"Jee-zuzz, why don't the pigs eat them? What kind of stuff is it a pig won't eat?

Parker took the walking-sticks to the second cell in the back. There were only two cells and Vanderland was in the other one.

"We've got to get you out of here," Parker said. "I can't put anyone in this cell with the sticks and how would you like it if we pick up three or four drunks and put them in with you?"

"Where can I go? My old man doesn't want me."

"I can't very well put you up at the College Inn. The Mayor wouldn't like spending that money. I guess I'll have to send you over the Notch to Holford."

"What? I've heard about the cells there, they're full of low class criminals."

Parker stood still and silent, wondering what to do. He got an idea.

He knew it would drive Davy up the wall. The Mayor also might not be keen. Still . . .

"You were an almost all right part-time cop," he said.

"Yeah?"

"I could drop the charge of shooting me. Do you have any more cocaine?"

"Do I look like I got Frankincense on me?"

"We could forget that too. That only leaves stealing a car and stealing some clothes in Vermont. I could probably get you out of that."

"What's the angle?"

"You come back working here."

"Are you kidding?"

This was echoed by Davy when Parker told him.

"You're off your chump, Boomer."

Then he thought how the Mayor could easily get rid of loony Boomer now. Davy would wear the top cop's badge. The babes would be begging for it. He might not have to tip the waitresses so much anymore.

Earl P. Vanderland happened to phone the station just then.

Parker told him the news.

"You mean you're actually going to pay that low life moron money?" Earl P. said.

Parker began to see what had gone wrong with young Vanderland.

"Do you have a mother?" he asked him.

"Sure I got a mother. What do you think, I was made in a jar in the cellar?"

"Where is she?"

"Working on her fourth husband somewhere. Number three didn't work out, he didn't have the sort of money she likes."

Good God, all that and a diet of fish jam and pigs' leavings. It was a wonder young Vanderland turned out as well as he did, Parker thought.

"You're going to have trouble with him, Boomer," Davy said, and he smiled when he said it. Bughouse, he said to himself, Boomer has gone bughouse. Davy's lot was a happy one today.

22

Trouble came. Parker had a reason for freeing Young Vanderland, but he started to doubt it.

I should have stuck to being a lawyer, he said to himself, and then he remembered that he hadn't actually made a living being a lawyer because everyone thought he was crazy; or at least half crazy. Also his third of the Appleseed bookstore was not bringing in the big bucks.

The problem now was where should Vanderland live.

Earl P. didn't want to take him in. Parker already had Sue and the Captain Elmo fan living in his house. The College Inn was too expensive.

There were some horrible rooms in the attic at the Lake House that nobody ever stayed in.

Parker got Vanderland fixed up there.

He told Vanderland that he wanted him on the night shift at the station.

"Can I bring a girl in?"

"What girl have you got in mind? Margot Cuncliffe?"

"I've seen enough of her."

"You've seen all of her."

"I was thinking of Mimi, I was wondering what she does to make men kill themselves."

*

Parker was wondering the same thing. He was also getting more suspicious of the people at Gledhill. One of them had committed murder. He wasn't doing his job letting whoever it was get away with it. Something's got to be done, he said to himself. But what? he answered.

The old DeSoto knew the way to Gledhill by itself.

There was bright sunlight but it was colder than ever. The bare branches of the trees were covered with ice. It no longer looked like the end of the world. This was a fairy land.

But there was at least one demon fairy at the big house.

The DeSoto pulled up at the front entrance even though it looked like it should go to a back door.

Moll came with Parker.

There was still a Christmas wreath on the door. A pergola covered with wisteria at the side of the house had yellow, red and blue lights ready to be turned on in the evening.

Edward was behaving as though nothing bad had happened at Gledhill. The much decorated tree was still in the hall. Edward obviously wasn't going to take the decorations down until Twelfth Night, the evening of January 5. That was the tradition. It fitted his character, or at least the character he wanted to show.

Maud Brewster answered the door. She should have been in the kitchen but from what Parker heard it was best to keep her out of there.

She wasn't pleased to see Parker. Her face was aggressively thin and there was something dangerous about how slim she was, as if she might suddenly biteth like a serpent.

Being so thin showed she was wise enough not to eat her own cooking Parker thought.

"Who's in the kitchen?" he asked.

Maud blinked at the sudden question.

"A Mrs Jane Hopkins," she said. "She insisted on it. I'm in there, however, as much as I can be."

"To keep her from stealing the spoons?" Parker said.

*

Jane was cooking meatloaf. Someone came in.

"Hello, old girl," Jane said.

Moll barked a greeting.

Jane gave her a slice of meatloaf and could see she had one satisfied customer.

Parker entered.

Jane was bent down patting Moll. "Who's a cute girl Mollster?" she said.

Just because she loves dogs doesn't mean she's not a killer, Parker told himself. Times were hard. Things were getting too cute. The whole scene was too cute. There had been people wearing ice-picks. Not cute that.

Parker and Moll went back to the front hall.

"Mr Burgess is in the library," Maud Brewster said.

Parker didn't want to see him. He wanted to think some more about Kindly Old Edward before seeing him.

"Where's Mimi Burgess?"

"Wandering around the house somewhere. If you shout for her she'll no doubt hear you."

Maud Brewster drooped away, a tall thin person who's decided she's done enough standing.

Moll went back to the kitchen.

Parker found Mimi in widow's wear in the glass extension.

A television had appeared among the sporting goods and foliage. It was turned on without the sound.

"I'm waiting to see if I'm in the news," Mimi said. "When you are looking at me," she said, "are you undressing me with your eyes?"

"I suppose I might if I didn't like what you were wearing. Then, I don't know much about clothes."

"I can see that. What about my eyes? Do they invite you to illegal pleasures?"

"Who are you?" he asked.

"Everybody knows who I am."

"But where do you come from?"

"Texas."

Parker was amazed. He didn't think Texas girls looked like Mimi.

"I'm trailer trash," she said. "We didn't have a dime. My mother was a waitress. I was a waitress. Grandma was a waitress too. That's why I'm so good at playing waitresses."

"What's this thing about waitresses? I was a waiter once."

"I dunno. It just is."

Parker started thinking maybe she wasn't actually mad. Perhaps only murderously eccentric.

"I played a rich high school girl once. I turned her into a real sex-mad tramp. I had a real good time doing that. I should have got an Oscar. Trouble there were eighty-six other movies just like it. Sexy high school tramps were big that year."

Mimi's face suddenly appeared on the television screen.

"Look at that," she said.

She turned the sound up.

"Sure they kill themselves out of love for me," she was saying on the screen.

There was laughter. Quite loud laughter.

"The bastards are laughing at me," Mimi shouted at the TV set. "I'll kill them. I'll get an ice pick and drive it into their necks."

*

Davy was a real cop. A cop's cop. Things were black or white – there were no various shades of gray.

Davy watched Parker treating Vanderland as if Vanderland were a real cop. Davy didn't like it. He left the station and drove round North Holford. It looked frozen white, like something that would never again see a Spring thaw and hear a baseball umpire shout "Play ball".

Gledhill, he thought, was the only place with the possibility of action. At least they were killing each other up there.

He rang the bell at the big house and that un-cook like lady opened the door.

She didn't look like a waitress either. She didn't look like anything connected to food.

She said, "What are you grinning at? Have you come to arrest anyone? Or simply to bore them to death with more idiotic questions?"

"You speak real good for a cook."

"I'm at Abigail Jefferson."

"You're the cook there?"

"I'm a professor."

"A prof, eh? What do you teach them?"

"Something worthwhile."

She looked like she was going to slam the door in his face.

And then she did slam the door.

Well, Davy thought, it can only get better.

On the other side of the door Maud said to herself, Maybe I told him too much. I shouldn't let anyone know who I am.

23

Sue was getting increasingly worried about her father's relationship with Mimi.

"God almighty," she said to Phyllis, "did you see what she was wearing? She got that skirt at Sluts-R-Us."

"I wouldn't worry about Parker."

Phyllis spoke from experience. She'd often been turned down by Parker. She changed the subject.

"Jimmy's leg is OK," she said.

"But where can he go? He'll have to stay here."

Jimmy the Brainiac was sitting on the big brown leather Chesterfield sofa. He wasn't reading Captain Elmo. He was reading Henry James, the book with the bullet hole in it.

*

Parker at this time was in the station with Davy.

"That new dame at Gledhill, Boomer, she ain't a real cook. She ain't even a make-believe cook, she's a prof."

"Where is she a prof?"

"Right here at Abigail Jefferson, teaching them spoiled brat rich kids something."

"What does she teach them?"

"She didn't tell me. She just said it was something worthwhile."

Parker sat thinking, then he said, "Alice Dickinson runs the press office at Abigail Jefferson. She'll know about Maud Brewster."

The press office sent releases to a student's local newspaper if the girl ever did anything interesting. Pregnancies, abortions, drug arrests and common drunkenness were not included.

Alice and Parker knew each other almost to the point of being friends.

Parker called her and asked what Maud Brewster taught at Abigail Jefferson.

"Art," Alice said, "and she does Gracious Living Evenings."

This taught the girls what knife, fork and spoon to use. Also how to be a hostess. The role of a wife was no longer underlined. Women's Liberation had hit Gracious Living pretty hard. It made Abigail Jefferson seem like a finishing school rather than a college. Still, most of the girls were as eager as their mothers had been to find rich men to support them.

"Has she been at Abigail Jefferson long?"

"No, she only came at the beginning of this year."

"Where's she from?"

"That's just it, she refused to tell me anything. She didn't want any publicity when we asked what her local newspaper was."

Parker didn't know how important Maud's arrival at Gledhill was, but it was suspicious. Kindly Old Uncle Edward had brought her there. Edward was getting to be a most suspicious character.

But Parker still couldn't see Edward putting ice picks in the necks of guests or a dagger in the back of a relative. But the loss of the late Old Uncle Andrew's gold coins and ornaments needed solving.

*

Earl P. Vanderland, the houseguest of Bruce Dane, was in a warm room filled with Dane's collection of gold objects. Bars had been put on the windows but it still had a view of cold winter.

Earl P. was observing Chief Daniels coming up to the house.

"Here comes that moron police chief," Earl P. said to Dane who was sitting on the other side of the room reading *Doubloon Quarterly*.

"Have you come about my boy Bob?" Earl P. said as Parker stepped into the room.

"Not particularly, I've got him working overnight. That's when it's quiet."

"Not much chance then of him shooting anyone. Or selling them dope."

Parker ignored Earl P.

"Mr Dane," he said, "I see you've put bars on the windows. Have you had any more calls from buyers?"

Dane reluctantly put down *Doubloon Quarterly*.

"I get calls all the time. Someone called this morning looking for gold dung beetles."

"Good God!" Earl P. said.

"We usually call them scarabs. This caller didn't. He sounded odd. His voice was like a boy's."

"Did he give a name?" Parker said.

"Let me see, it was odd –"

"Bichard?"

"That's right. James Rutherford Bichard. How did you know?"

Parker didn't let Dane know.

"Is he a well-known collector?" Earl P. asked.

"Not by me," Dane said.

"He's known to the police," Parker said.

Earl P. looked surprised.

"You're obviously on the ball, Chief. I must say it comes as a surprise, after that stunt freeing my boy Bob. Bob takes after his mother's side of the family, which is surprising because his mother ran away when he was seven."

Parker was thinking that Young Vanderland looked just like his father, behaved like him, talked like him, and thought like him, minus the greed for gold.

"You shouldn't have freed him," Earl P. said. "His mother ought to get locked up too."

He stood very tall, with a frown on his brow and with a look in his eyes as if he were going to shout at someone.

Parker made an excuse and left the room.

❊

It was time to see how bonkers Mimi was today.

Parker thrust the old DeSoto at Gledhill. He was halfway up Memory Hill when Ottoline appeared, marching up the snowy slope in her British walkers with laces.

He gave her a lift. Moll got in the back.

"I'm going to see Mimi," he said.

"Me too. I want to know if she had anything to do with Jack's murder."

Gledhill was still looking like an expensive Christmas card.

The door was opened by the tall hardly there Maud.

"Oh brother," Ottoline said under her breath.

"Mr Daniels," Maud said in a most superior tone, "you will give this residence a bad name if you continue this police procession."

Parker thought murders and a suspicious suicide had already reduced the market value.

"I can't imagine what the neighbours think," Maud said.

Ottoline said, "There aren't any neighbours."

"I don't wish to stand here explaining it to you, miss."

"Missis. I'm the Widow Smith."

Maud gazed at Ottoline with an expression that said it was exceptionally vulgar for a widow to have such a common name.

Parker almost had to demand entrance.

His search for Mimi was stopped by Bill Summers.

The prep school teacher and football coach, was with a young man whom Parker recognized as Jake the nephew.

"Is this another daughter?" Jake said.

If Parker was going to say anything he didn't have a chance. Ottoline said, "How stupid are you, boy?"

Jake fell back at being assaulted by such a British accent calling him "boy".

Summers said, "Your Sergeant Shea is upstairs somewhere giving my former fiancée, Margot, the Third Degree. I wish he would get her off my back!"

Ottoline answered for Parker.

"That's immensely riveting," she said, "but we are looking for that tragic figure, Mimi of the Movies."

"Are you in the local police now?" Summers said.

"I'm an amateur sleuth. Maybe a gumshoe. Where, by the way," she said to Maud, "is the Widow Burgess?"

"I'm sure I don't know," Maud said, as if knowing Mimi's whereabouts was like knowing the way to the laundry.

"Say, sister," Ottoline said with a linguistic leap into mobster speak, "what do you do except open doors?"

"I teach art at Abigail Jefferson College."

"No kidding? I was at the Courtauld Institute and worked in a gallery in London until the late Smith rescued me."

Maud took cover in a dissyllable.

"Indeed!" she said.

Ottoline laughed, which Maud hadn't meant her to do.

"I suppose Mimi is hiding out in that extension with all the glass, golf clubs, skis and hockey sticks," Parker said.

Parker walked through the house to the extension. Ottoline and Summers and nephew trailed behind.

There was a rare winter fly in the room. It saw sunlight and attempted to get to it; if only the air would stop being so difficult to get through. It didn't understand glass and was trying to fly through it. Obviously it also didn't understand snow or it wouldn't be so anxious to get outside.

Mimi was in tears.

"It's my nerves," she said, "I think I'm going mad."

She held onto her head as if she were afraid it might fall off.

Parker thought Mimi no longer funny. She was a pathetic figure.

He was worried she might do herself some injury. He looked for a knife.

There was something even more sinister – an ice pick.

24

Mimi, seated with her legs tucked under her in a yoga position, looked up at Parker.

The rose-lipped Mimi was also the red-eyed Mimi. She had been weeping and she looked like she was going to deliver further scattered showers.

When she saw Parker she started to talk as if the power of speech had just come to her.

A phantasmagoria emerged of real and imaginary men who had loved her; an entire regiment of the love-struck. He wouldn't be surprised if Mark Anthony, Romeo and Frank Sinatra were mentioned.

"Nick loved me," she said, adding for perhaps the hundredth time, "you know, he killed himself because I loved another."

"An unhappy event," Parker said.

"I thought Donald Billings loved me," she said.

She got to her feet. She had the ice pick in her hand. It looked at home there and this worried the police chief of a small New England town in which the usual lawbreakers were drivers who parked in restricted areas during the daylight hours.

"He betrayed me," Mimi said. "You can understand that can't you?"

Parker was silent, his eyes on the ice pick.

"Perhaps you can't understand a man betraying me. You love me too much to believe any man could betray me, don't you?"

Parker said nothing.

Mimi said, "You are madly in love with me, aren't you? You should get someone else to interview me. It must be terribly painful for you. Love is hell."

"I've been meaning to talk to you about that."

"I know, I know, you are being driven insane by it."

"Not quite."

It was the wrong thing to say.

"What?" she said. "What?" she repeated as if talking to a mynah bird who wasn't mimicking the word properly.

"What makes you think I love you?" Parker said.

"I was coming downstairs and I swore that the next man I saw I would make love me."

The red-eyes of the previously weeping Mimi traveled over Parker's face to see what reaction this was having. Dumbfounded seemed good enough to her.

"I'm terribly sorry," he said.

"Don't be. I may love you back someday when there's no one else around."

"I mean I don't love you. As lovable as you obviously are you are not the object of my affections."

He had come to Gledhill to see how bonkers Mimi was.

He now found out.

She sprang at him.

Luckily Parker was so tall she did not succeed in putting the ice pick in the region of preference. It missed his neck but went into his left shoulder.

Mimi pulled it out and was ready to strike again. She felt she must tell him what she planned.

"I'm going to kill you," she said. "Donald Billings didn't love me and I killed him. Now I'll kill you."

Parker wondered if the situation required him to hit a woman. He thought it did.

He didn't have to.

The door flew open and Summers fell into the room, pushed by his nephew Jake, Davy and Ottoline.

Summers performed a football tackle on Mimi.

She went down and Ottoline stood on her ice pick arm.

Davy produced handcuffs and fastened her arms behind her.

Parker was standing leaning back on a pair of skis, looking at the blood from his shoulder.

"Cuff her in front, Davy," he said. "It'll be more comfortable for her in the car."

"Comfortable for her, Boomer? Look at yourself."

"We've got to get her to the County jail. We can't accommodate her in the station," Parker said.

Ottoline came and stood face to face with Mimi.

"Why did you kill Jack?" she said.

"Who?" Mimi said.

"Jack, my husband."

"Oh, was his name Jack? I didn't know. He wasn't important. He just walked in on me when I was paying off Donald."

Parker thought he should thank them all, and especially Summers for saving his life with the tackle.

"Dr Skypeck will have to see you," Ottoline said to the still bleeding Parker.

*

Well, it's all over now, Boomer, ice picks for them two and a fancy dagger with jewels for Old Man Andrew. It all fits."

"Has she confessed to putting the knife in Andrew?"

"Maybe she don't remember."

"Who's got the gold?" Parker said.

Davy seemed to have forgotten the one thousand, six hundred and fifty-eight dollars and twenty cents an ounce of gold was selling for.

Parker made his painful way out of Gledhill.

Maud looked at him as if she were going to tell him to stop bleeding on the floor.

State Police Captain Inez Bodegus and Sergeant O'Brien were taking Mimi to her command performance at the County jail.

The press were at Gledhill, spread out like litter on the drive.

Hapless Jones, Johnny Peru and Vince Vanilla were among the scribes.

Mimi, however, attempted to get her face into Blondie Barrack's TV camera.

She struck a dramatic pose. She was no longer playing a waitress. She had got herself into Major League drama. Oscars went to stuff like this.

"Any minute now," Ottoline said, "she's going to mention Mr DeMille."

Mimi was a sad figure.

"She won't go to prison," Parker said. "She'll be in a hospital. She's pregnant. She might even get well and get back in the movies."

Ottoline was worried by this view of what might be Mimi's future.

But Parker was getting pale. In fact paler and paler. He looked as if he might suddenly fade away like the Cheshire cat in *Alice in Wonderland*.

Ottoline said, "We've got to get you to Doc Skypeck. She's waiting at your house."

*

"Luckily, Dr Phyllis said, "it's not deep."

She patched the shoulder.

Parker put on his mixed heather heirloom tweed coat.

"What do you look like?" said the pretty English widow.

"I've no idea. Maybe you could tell me."

"I suppose shabby chic might cover it."

"I don't want the chic, I seek only the shabby."

"You've got it."

"I won't give it away, no matter how they clamber for it."

Dr Phyllis was not much amused by this mutual "hitting on".

Daughter Sue thought it good for Pop Boomer's often much ragtailed persona. But the pretty Smith woman had so recently been made a widow, was it proper?

God, Sue thought, I sound like my Mother!

The pretty widow Smith looked about. She did not seem much pleased.

She said, "I'm not at all pleased by the snow at this moment, it comes with wind and is so cold. Not at all romantic."

"What would you call romantic? In what season would that be?" Sue said.

"The summer. In the summer you have the luxury of shade."

"Not sun?"

"Not sun, it is so common. Shade is not vulgar. And is it not nice to sit in the shade under a tree and remember love?"

Her gray blue eyes turned on Boomer. Was there the hope of memories to come in that gaze? Sue asked herself.

*

Parker was in the news. Mayor Snow thought it might be good for North Holford's image if Parker was spruced up sartorially.

Ottoline was of similar mind. "The trouble is," she said, "there's only one place for male toggery in North Holford."

Sue, who was beginning to like Ottoline, said, "It's not much of a place, Jack Montana's Tog Shop. All the suits look like they come with a deck of cards."

They found an old tweed sports jacket that Parker's wife had bought him in an early week of wedded bliss. The coat now looked like the moths had fired a shotgun at it, but it would have to do.

Parker arrived at the station and Mayor Snow started to speak.

He painted a hideous word-picture of mental Mimi.

"Is it all over, Mr Mayor?" Vince Vanilla asked.

"You betcha," Mayor Snow said. "We are now back being a hub of winter entertainment."

"Look this way and say that again," Blondie Barrack said.

Blondie's camelhair coat was opened from neck to knee, displaying an extravagant blue indigo female seascape. The face, however, was still stupid in the way only much made-up minor celebrity faces can be.

"What about you, Chief?" someone shouted.

Parker pretended not to hear.

He thought it would be answered pretty soon, written in blood.

25

Bill Summers dropped in to see how the life he had saved was getting on.

Parker now saw that Summers was a good-looking male specimen. Parker had heard of the girls at Cheshire Academy getting a crush on him; and of affairs with female teachers – all the female teachers. And a man who could get engaged to the half-clad Margot was a man with an unhealthy interest in romance.

Parker got up to leave. He was thinking of going to Sam's Spaghetti House for dinner.

"I'm off to Sam Righetti's," he said.

He was going to sit there at Sam's and think about what the hell was going to happen next.

*

It was happening right then, at the colonial-replica home of Bruce "Brucie" Dane, the grocery magnate and gatherer of gold.

Dane finished reading *Doubloon Quarterly*. Earl P. was out somewhere. Rosie was busy at Sam Righetti's serving spaghetti, macaroni, vermicelli, pizza or Pizza Pizazz (a speciality of Sam's) and burgers (nutburgers for the vegetarians).

With Rosie missing Brucie was going to dine alone. At least he thought he was.

He had a TV dinner, from one of his own supermarkets. He wasn't sure what was in it. The contents label looked like a snap chemistry quiz.

There was a sudden cold draught at the 18th century colonial-replica dining-room table.

I forgot to close the window, he said to himself.

What was happening was someone was opening one.

Brucie felt the cold draught on his neck.

*

Phyllis drove to Codere's Grove Wine & Dine, the weary wooden structure perched over the water on the tough side of the lake where the inordinate poor pretended to live.

The Grove was erected in the 1930s and had been there ever since, with only four new roofs, three new walls and only two new foundations. It was almost historic.

Phyllis's father, Fred Skypeck and the Warsaw Polka Boys, were performing.

Leonardo Vitonelli, who clearly wasn't anything near Polish, was on the bandstand singing the best he could in Polish.

He had the words of the song (about a steamboat) written down for him in Polish on a sheet of paper so he could read it while attempting to sing.

No one in the audience, however Polish their names, could speak the language of their great grandfathers. They didn't know any more than Leonardo about what he was singing. The Great Melting Pot had done its work on them.

This went for the band too, with the exception of Fred Skypeck; and Phyllis, a clever girl, she could read and speak five languages, including the Latin of Ovid.

She looked around for someone who could dance the polka.

Chuck Newberry, a local garage mechanic, was lounging against the lattice-work screen on the side of a booth.

Phyllis had removed a pesky cyst from his backside last July and charged him next to nothing, which was what Chuck charged her for working on her car.

Phyllis nodded at him and he reluctantly moved towards the dance floor.

"I don't know how good I'll be performing an Old World Folk Dance," he said.

"I'm Old World Folk enough for both of us. I'll lead, you just have to jump a bit."

She wasn't at ease doing the polka either. She did it to please Pop Skypeck, trying to hide the embarrassing awkwardness she felt.

There was something wrong, Leonardo's Polish wasn't up to much, he seemed to be singing about ecto-zoon. As an ectozoon was a parasite that lives on the outside of its host, Phyllis thought he must be getting it wrong.

"What's Vitonelli singing about?" Chuck asked.

"A thing that latches on to you and starts eating you."

"Love, huh?

Chuck was a mechanic who knew more than machinery could go wrong. A broken heart had driven him to Codere's Wine & Dine this evening.

Phyllis he knew wasn't for him. She, he thought, was the kind of girl who might want to sit down of an evening and talk Latin. He couldn't see her taking an interest in his love life. His backside was the only part of him that had ever interested her. Of course, when you had a cyst on your rear end love did not seem important.

Vitonelli's musical ordeal ended, a round of applause showed emphatic approval of the musical conclusion.

The dance over Phyllis thought of Parker. He didn't do the polka any better than Chuck Newberry but it was fun with Parker.

Thinking of Parker she didn't like seeing him with that pretty English woman, Ottoline Smith. But maybe the Widow Smith was a suspect. Of course she was. Mr Smith was murdered. Mimi confessed to killing him, but maybe the self-obsessed movie star was bragging. There was talk of taking Mimi out of the County jail and putting her in the Convent of the Little Sisters of St. Rita, Patron Saint of Impossible Dreams, in nearby Bluefield. Father Cortez at the Church of St. John the Cousin was suggesting this. St. Rita's handled loonies.

Phyllis's phone rang. It was Parker.

Good Lord, she thought when she got the message – another dead man!

Dr Stanley Howse, the first-string police surgeon, was otherwise occupied with gin and vermouth this Yuletide. Phyllis was doing the corpses this season.

She blew a kiss to Fred and left the Grove for the home of the late Brucie Dane.

*

Rosie from Sam Righetti's Spaghetti House had discovered the body; trade had been bad this winter evening and she had left early, heading for Brucie's and the possibility of a heart-throbbing evening.

Brucie was, as Captain Inez would say, among the "former people" when Rosie arrived.

There was a number written down on the table by the house phone. "Call me here," it said.

She called and no one answered. She called several times more and someone finally answered.

It was Earl P. Vanderland.

"You ain't no cop," Rosie said.

"I'd rather be dead," Earl P. said. "Not even the cops want to be cops if they've got any ambition."

"Well," Rosie said, "I got someone who is dead right here."

"Who and where?"

"Your roomie, my Brucie." There was a sob.

"The only cop here is my boy Bob and he's sound asleep. I've been trying to wake him for more than half an hour. You got any idea what half an hour of my time is worth?"

That's when Rosie called Parker at his house.

And that was how Phyllis was invited to view yet another dead man.

Dane had been shot in the back of the head.

He might have been a contortionist, but there was no gun and no note. Suicide seemed not in the scenario.

26

The gold was gone. The colonial replica was searched by Parker and Davy, with help from Inez and O'Brien.

They went from the ice cavern cellar to the attic which contained replica antique dust and cobwebs but no gold; and then out to the garage. The Danemobile parked there was turned upside down and shaken. Nothing.

"Well," Parker said, "all we have to do is find who's got the gold."

"Is that going to be easy, Boomer?"

"A lot easier than if he was killed by someone who did it for fun."

"For fun?"

"For the hell of it."

Davy noted again Parker's decline into whimsy. Any moment now he would become so eccentric that even Mayor Snow might notice it.

"We should find the gun," Davy said.

"It'll have been wiped clean, but it would look dramatic in court."

More whimsy, Davy mentally jotted it down.

"Where's the bullet?" Davy asked Phyllis.

"Where someone put it. In his head."

"Can you get it out?"

"I'll have to get the body to the morgue at Holford City Hospital."

An ambulance arrived. "Where is it?" a medic said.

"OK," Parker said to the medic, "you can take him away. He's Bruce Dane, he has a name. He's not it."

"The deceased is nice," Phyllis said. "Or maybe the dear departed."

Davy thought they had things to do. At least one thing to do.

"Let's get Earl P. Vanderland. He's the obvious suspect."

Rosie sprang to attention.

"It can't be him," she said, "when I found Brucie dead I called the police station and he answered the phone."

"Who answered the phone?"

"Earl P. answered the phone."

Just then the hall door opened and Earl P. walked into the circa 1776 style dining-room.

"You missed the *corpus delicti*," Davy said. "Or maybe you seed him already."

"*Corpus delicti?*" said Earl P., who had had Latin as well as money included in his liberal humanistic education.

"Yeah sure, Jack, that's right."

"If you say so," Earl P. said.

"You bet I do, George."

"It's Earl."

"What is?"

"My name."

"Who says it ain't? This guy's the killer, Boomer. Let's take him down and lock him up. He's got money, he's the kind of guy who will take it on the lam to Brazil or Costa Rica."

"What were you doing at the station, Mr Vanderland?" Parker said.

"Trying to wake up my boy Bob, the half wit; he takes after his mother's side of the family."

"He was asleep? I thought he wouldn't be too wide awake, but being sound asleep was more than I could have hoped for."

Davy was full of wonder, puzzled by this latest edition of whimsy.

Hapless Jones from the *Holford Evening Transcript,* came into the room.

"Say," Parker said, "I've got an amusing angle on this."

He told Hapless about young Vanderland being asleep.

Johnny Peru and Vince Vanilla came into the room.

"Asleep, huh?" Peru said.

"You mean sleeping? Sleep sleeping?" Vanilla said.

"That's right," Parker said.

Peru and Vanilla scribbled down this libel on the North Holford police.

"This Vanderland is the same punk who shot you?" Peru said.

"The dope peddler?" Vanilla said.

The journalistic duo, like Davy, started thinking that Parker was letting whimsy get into his head and take over.

"What are you up to?" Peru said.

"Oh nothing," Parker said.

"You're up to something," Vanilla said.

He was but he wasn't going to tell them.

"Hey," Hapless said, "how do most people spell Vanderland?"

*

Bob Vanderland found his latest claim to fame worrying.

"What are they going to think of me?"

"They'll think you should have slept during the day time," Parker said.

"I tried. I couldn't do it."

It was daylight now and Bob Vanderland was wide awake.

"Am I still on overnights?"

"It's the best place for you."

Summers and his nephew came into the station.

"I'm being nosey," Bill Summers said.

Summers no longer looked romantic. He was back to looking sinister. Jake, the nephew, however, was still looking lovelorn.

"You're not locking up Earl P.?" Summers asked.

"Not today."

"Not any day, if Boomer has his way."

"Is Sue still in North Holford?" Jake asked.

"Until Twelfth Day," Parker said. He thought he had told this to Jake before.

"When's that?" the boy said.

He was like someone who thought he might miss the 3.10 on Track 29 at Grand Central and kept asking the time.

"You'll be sure to recognize it," Parker said, "there will be eight lords aleaping, five golden rings and other things."

Jee-zuzz, Davy said to himself. Summers continued looking sinister. Inez Bodegus came in.

"You ain't arrested no one, Boomer? You got criminals playing cop and the only suspect in the Dane slaying is driving around free in a champagne colored Cadillac."

Davy didn't like Inez. But he went along with her on this. She could be a witness when they had Boomer up for whimsicality at the Town Hall Meeting.

"A partridge in a pear tree," Parker said to Lovelorn Jake, "that's another thing to look out for."

Davy whistled in amazement.

The front window had been left open when Parker had looked out. Now, only a second after Davy's whistle, there was an amazing performance. Flying through the window came Moll. She was a dog who couldn't, even without a whistle, resist an open window.

"What's that?" Summers said.

"My dog," Parker said.

"What's her name?" Jake said.

"Miss Sheherazade Old Compton Gun Moll, but that's only when she goes out to Junior League Cotillions. She's just Moll when she's being informal."

"I've seen the dog before," Jake said.

"I haven't," Summers said.

"Yes, you have," Jake said.

"Shut up about the damn dog," his uncle said.

*

Davy left the station and headed west to Gledhill.

It was Gloomy Gledhill today under a black sky. The festive decorations did nothing to help. Even the sparrows in the eaves had given up and weren't chirping today.

The knife-thin Maud Brewster answered the door. She looked at Davy with eyes that wanted to turn him to stone.

"What are you doing here?" Davy asked.

"Standing looking at a moron."

"Moron?"

"Well, dull normal."

"I mean why are you in Gledhill if you ain't the cook?"

"Gracious living," she said. "I can't teach the girls about gracious living while I'm living in a pokey room in a dismal dormitory on campus."

She seemed to sag, as if this speech before a dull normal was too much for her.

Davy decided to seek out the flame-haired scarcely clad Margot.

Since Jane Hopkins had taken over the cooking there was no longer health reasons for missing meals at Gledhill.

Davy went to the kitchen to see if Margot was there. She wasn't; only Jane, whirling a wooden spoon in a saucepan, all the while singing to herself.

"I'm sorry to spoil things with cheerfulness," she said, "but I've had good news."

"Oh?" Davy said.

"I've found a restaurant I can buy just outside Philadelphia. Or at least Stephen found it for me."

"That's nice. Have you seen Margot?"

"No, I'm afraid not."

Davy left the kitchen. He found Vita Cuncliffe.

"Margot left," she said. "I don't know where she went. She said she couldn't stand being in a haunted house."

"There ain't never no such thing."

"Tell that to the ghosts she hears banging around every night."

"Do you hear them too?"

"Not after half a bottle of claret at dinner, two martinis before, a brandy after, plus maybe eight martinis and a glass of warm milk at bed time. Ghosts can throw furniture around all night long and they won't wake me."

"Do you know where she's gone?"

"I haven't a clue. But she's sex mad. If you hear a woman wailing for her demon lover, that'll be Margot."

27

The missing Margot was in a taxi. Bart Laporte, the cab driver, built like an all-in wrestler, thought that soon he was going to be forced, if he was going to get anywhere, to get out and throw his taxi over the snowdrifts in the road.

That was the question, Bart thought, to get where?

The little lady, who looked like she had been seeing spooks, had come out of Gledhill with her mouth opened in case she needed to scream.

"I got twenty-three dollars and eighty-three cents," she said, "get me as far away from this place as twenty bucks will take me. That'll leave me three dollars and eighty-three cents for my old age."

Bart had already gone more than twenty bucks worth, but she was a damsel in distress. All his life he had wanted to meet one of those and this one was a distressed damsel worth looking at in the rear-view mirror. He supposed he should be looking at the snow clothed road ahead. But then, he said to himself, there ain't nothing out there I want to see.

A lazy winter dawn was trying to poke its nose out from under the snowy covers. If it had its way it would have stayed in bed.

"Miss," Bart said, "I can't just drop you off in a blizzard."

"Maybe we'll find a house that will take me in."

If there's an eager guy alone in the house he'll let her in all right, Bart said to himself. He was also an eager guy but at home there was a Mrs Bart, also put together like an all-in-wrestler.

"There's a house," Margot shouted, pointing a finger at a dark outline in the snow. "Or is it only a shadow?"

"It can't be no shadow," Bart said, "You got to have sun to have a shadow and we ain't got no sun."

As a weather report that seemed to cover it. Nevertheless, Bart knew a house was there and what's more he knew who lived in it.

"Just a sec," he said and dismounted and waded through three feet of snow to the door.

It was opened by a tall, lean, athletic-looking man.

"Coot," Bart said, "I got a damsel in distress in the back of my cab. Will you take her in? She's a looker."

Coot said he would. Or he nodded; a man of few words.

Bart went back to the cab and plucked Margot out. He carried her with one arm and her luggage with the other.

Margot ceased being frightened, she was now only lugubrious, which she thought was obviously dismal enough to have such a long word to describe it. She was put down in an armchair in front of a big log fire and she fell asleep.

Bart was a gentleman. He didn't wake her to get his twenty bucks.

Several hours later Margot was awake. She didn't actually know where she was. But she liked it. The fire was still burning. The room was excessively cozy. Gledhill wasn't cozy. It wasn't comfortable and it wasn't warm, and never would you call Gledhill snug and friendly.

Chez Coot was. Coot was a tall almost good-looking mysterious stranger.

"Who are you?" Coot asked.

"You know I'm not quite sure. I know who I was yesterday and maybe the day before that."

"And now?"

"Somebody else. Somebody I don't really know; that I couldn't possibly know, at least very well, because she's entirely new to me."

"Well, forget it. Don't worry yourself none. You been in a slump. I was in one for three months once. I couldn't hit a thing," said Coot, a former long-ball hitter for the New York Yankees.

Margot had little notion of what he was talking about. But she liked him. Part of the mystery for Margot was how dirty he was. Before she realized it Margot was saying something she had never said before.

"I'll wash your shirt."

"It's all right," the mystery man said, "I got another one. Trouble is I hung it out to dry and it froze. I've got it standing upside down in the bathroom thawing out. Want to see it?"

Margot surprised herself by saying she'd love to. She followed Coot upstairs. She saw why she was eager to see the frozen shirt standing on its own two arms in the bath tub. The bathroom was next door to the bedroom and she could remember that she was a girl who knew her way around one of those.

"I get dirty in the business I'm in these days," Coot said.

"Are you a coal miner?"

"Pretty close. I mine slate. Trouble is there's not much call for it. In my great-grandfather's day it was different. The Notch was cut out of the mountain to get slate. There's no money in it today. A man depending on it is poor."

"I don't think I'd mind a man being poor."

Again Margot surprised herself. She remembered that she was what Eastsodom, Long Island, called high class. A high class prep school, a high class college followed by London, Paris and Rome. Summers in the Sodoms and winters on Swiss slopes.

Where have they got you? she asked. Drugged with a runny nose in a haunted house full of dead bodies.

She gazed briefly at the Coot person. Why shouldn't she try a member of the proletariat? Granny Cuncliffe was no longer alive to drop down dead at the news.

"You know," she said, "I'm a floozy."

It was a word old-fashioned enough to almost sound respectable. At least it was comic.

"That's all right," he said. "I was Coot Williams."

"Who are you now?"

"Just about the same, but I didn't hit no forty homeruns anywhere this season. In fact, I don't hit no runs nowhere."

"I don't mind," she said.

She thought baseball players swinging bats about were something like lumberjacks. Granny had owned a forest in Oregon until a cousin of hers drank it away; along with the steel mill in Pittsburg.

"You know," she said, "I think I'm falling in love with you. In fact, I am in love with you."

Coot Williams, the strong silent type, managed to say, "That's OK."

Margot felt like calling Vita and telling her, but ghosts might be listening and come to get her.

"I was in San Francisco," Coot said, "and then St Louis, Cleveland, Baltimore and finally New York."

"You had trouble settling down?"

"With New York I was only a pinch hitter. Then I was all done. I came back to the slate."

And he was a poor man because of it, she thought. She still didn't mind. It was good that they would be poor. Whenever they got some extra money it would be such a pleasure.

"May I stay here?" she said.

"OK," the strong silent former pinch hitter said.

"I don't mind at all if we're poor," she said.

"Me neither," Coot said. "Trouble was I was playing ball when we were struggling along even in the Majors on a lousy million a year. That was the average way back then."

"A million what?"

"Bucks," the strong silent Coot told her.

Good Lord, she thought, he's not the poor man of my dreams. An average of a million a year in the Majors and he had been there twenty years.

She would try not to hold that against him. Love conquers all, she told herself.

✻

Davy was in the station telling Parker what was what with the missing Margot.

"She always was a part-time loco," he said, "but now she's gone full time."

"It was ghosts she said she heard?" Parker asked.

"Yeah. Gone absolute bugs."

Georgie said, "My aunt Lucy heard the ghost of my late Uncle Reg talking to her one night. Then she found out he wasn't a late. He was run off to Kansas City, Kansas with the lady from the dry cleaners. She only had one leg so I suppose we shouldn't say run off."

Parker and Davy ignored Georgie's relatives.

"We've got to find her," Parker said.

"Who, the lady from the dry cleaners?" Georgie said.

"Margot."

"What's she got to do with anything important?" Davy said.

"She might have. Did anyone else hear anything?"

"Vita was too tanked. I didn't ask no others."

"I think I might do that. I'm going back to Gledhill."

The old DeSoto gave a weary sigh and turned its radiator up Memory Hill yet again.

The sky was just as black and low as it had been when Parker last went there. Gledhill was also as gloomy. He made his way through two and a half feet of snow to the front door. It was answered by the unwelcoming Maud.

"Margot's not here," she said, "I don't know where she is and I don't care."

28

Gledhill was so cold Parker could see his own breath coming out in plumes of white smoke. In the library the part of the rose red and peacock blue Persian carpet nearest the window was white with frost.

Somebody, he said to himself, wants everyone to leave.

That somebody would have to be Edward. He owned the house now. He controlled the room temperature.

Parker followed the white plumes of his breath to the kitchen which was warm and which was full of everyone, with the exception of the tall thin Maud.

"Listen," Parker said, "Margot is missing. She must have left the house in some sort of vehicle. Are all the cars still here?"

Edward went out to count the cars in the drive.

"They're hard to see under all the snow," he said when he came back, "but they all seem to be there."

"What about the garage?" Parker said. He knew at least a dozen cars would fit in there.

"There's only a broken down tractor in there," Edward told him. "And an old Stutz Bearcat that hasn't worked since 1934."

The antique car was another item of value in Gledhill. About half a million dollars worth, Parker thought.

Parker felt sorry for Edward staggering through snow counting cars. To save him another stroll in the blizzard Parker went to the garage.

There was something that looked like parts of a Stanley Steamer spread out on the floor. Also a 1914 Rolls Royce that looked like it should have a horse in front of it. A Benz, before Mercedes got her name on it; a Maxwell, a Hudson, and a Packard that looked like it should come with gangsters with Chicago typewriters. There was a big 1929 Cadillac that still worked. Parker didn't know anything about any car except the DeSoto, but he could see there was something odd about this old Caddie. It had a speaking tube from the backseat to the driver. There was something wrong about the speaking tube. Then he guessed – it was made of gold. The headlights and the grill also seemed to be made of gold. Ditto the fenders and hubcaps. At the price of gold today a big chunk of Andrew's ten million was in this golden chariot, but the Mystery of the Missing Margot was the chief subject now.

Parker came stamping his feet back through the garden-room to the kitchen.

"Only museum pieces," he said. "Margot got away either on foot or in a cab."

After asking about bumps in the night, to which he got no good answers, Parker headed back to the police station to call Bart Laporte.

"Sure I picked up the kid," Bart said. "She was talking about ghosts and she only had twenty three dollars and eighty three cents on her. I found a place for her."

Bart was reluctant to say where, then Parker mentioned that this was a murder investigation.

"Coot Williams," Bart said.

"Coot Williams," Parker said.

"Coot Williams?" Davy said. "In his day he reminded me of Lou Gehrig."

"Of the 1927 New York Yankees?" Parker said. "You never saw Lou Gehrig play."

"Yeah, but I seen an actor play him in a movie."

North Holford had two former Major League baseball players. The other was Whitey Gotton on the far side of the lake in Old Compton. He had two twenty-game seasons with the Red Sox before he was sold to Los Angeles where he burned up the league until his shoulder went.

"I'm going to Coot Williams' place," Parker said.

Both Davy and Georgie looked eagerly at Parker. Young Vanderland was also there, instead of in bed in the Lake House, but he was un-American and didn't like baseball even though his father once came near to buying a team.

"I can't take both of you," Parker said, "and it would be unfair to take only one."

"We could flip a coin," Davy said.

He tossed one in the air calling heads. It was tails.

"Best of three," Davy said.

"That ain't right," Georgie said.

They started shouting. Parker left. He thought maybe he should have taken Young Vanderland to punish him for being out of bed.

But Parker wanted Vanderland where he was.

The DeSoto headed, with hardly a complaint, for Coot Williams.

*

Parker could smell the coffee as he climbed over the snow drifts to the front door of Coot's authentic New England colonial cottage.

A woman answered the door and Parker didn't recognize her. She was wearing an old-fashioned baseball warm-up jacket with an ancient and much worn gray sweater under it. The sweater was too big and hung down almost to her knees like a short skirt.

Then Parker recognized the flame red hair and the killer legs looking good even in high cut lumberjack boots.

"I've just made coffee," Margot said.

"Thanks," Parker said.

Not only Margot's costume but also her face was different. She was wearing several less layers of makeup. Gone was the glowing painted smile of a high class glamour girl.

Parker heard noise coming from just behind the back door.

"Coot's chopping wood," Margot said.

She thought that she could see that Parker was embarrassed seeing her wearing clothes rather than in her normal state of half undressed.

"Ask away," she said. "Coot knows everything. At least the everything that I chose to tell him. I got to save somethings for when we're old and gray."

"I want to know why you fled like you did from Gledhill."

"It's silly now to say it but I heard things go bump in the night."

"Did you go out to investigate?"

"Go out and ask the spooks what they thought they were doing? Are you kidding? I believed in ghosts then."

"You don't anymore?"

"Not here at least."

Parker knew what those ghosts were doing in Gledhill. They were prospecting for gold and moving it out of the house to some place where they could easily get their hands on it. Gledhill was chuckful of suspects. But how many were capable of hefting heavy bars of gold around?

He thought of Tom and Dick, the yardmen. They lived in a converted barn not far from Gledhill.

He left Margot in the happy home life and drove to Gledhill.

*

Tom and Dick were in but they were packing their bags preparing to leave. There should have been something suspicious about that.

Parker had seen them side by side for so long in North Holford that he had always thought of them as brothers. He was amazed when he found out they weren't. One of them was from Illinois, from Cicero, outside Chicago, and had a police record for small time stuff, nothing like murder.

Parker said, "It looks like you boys are taking it on the lam."

"Not us," Tom said. "We was sacked three or four days ago."

"Don't leave town," Parker said.

"Where are we supposed to stay?" Dick asked.

"We ain't got a dime," Tom said.

"Just a minute," Parker said.

He made a phone call in the next room.

"It's OK," he said when he came back. "Mrs Wilson across the street from me is over the flu and she's got a couple of spare rooms."

"Is she related to that Wilson kid?" Tom asked.

"Not that very much related."

"Who'd admit to it if they was?" Dick said.

They were going to Mrs Wilson's. With them only across the street Parker could keep an eye on them. But he had to keep watch on Gledhill before someone else was killed.

*

Darkness came early to a rural New England town.

Davy and Georgie kept looking at the clock to see when they could get off. After two dozen looks it was finally time.

Young Vanderland waited for them to leave and then pushed two desks together, climbed up and lay down preparing for a health restoring eight hours of, he hoped, pleasant dreams. He had had a beauty two days ago when he dreamt that he was an orphan.

There was, however, a tremendous noise outside. Someone was hammering on the door. Vanderland, gun in hand, went to investigate.

It was Jake Summers, drunk. This didn't surprise Vanderland. They were both college boys and college boys got drunk.

Jake fell into Vanderland's arms.

"Can't make it all the way back to the College Inn," Jake said. "Besides my uncle would kill me."

Vanderland thought if the uncle did kill him Jake would never feel it, but he hoisted him to the one remaining cell. The other cell was still being occupied by two dozen gold handled walking-sticks.

Vanderland hurried back to dreamland but he had only just got started drifting when there was further banging on the station door.

It was Jake's uncle, Big Bad Bill Summers, and he was in a mood.

"Jake," he said, "where is he?"

"He's in the back. In a cell."

"Let me see."

Vanderland led him to it.

Jake was stretched out in lounging posture. He sat up hearing the approaching footsteps and the jangling keys on a big key ring in Vanderland's hand.

When he saw his uncle, and that uncle was looking most unapproving, Jake stood up. The sight of the uncle made the nephew suddenly sober.

Vanderland was not surprised. Big Bad Bill would sober up a roomful of nephews.

He opened the cell door so the uncle could enter and kill the nephew.

Instead when the cell door was opened Vanderland was shoved in minus his gun and keys and Jake came out.

Big Bad Bill locked Vanderland in.

"You're every bit as stupid as you look," he said.

Summers and now completely sober nephew unlocked the other cell.

They started to collect the walking-sticks.

Summers turned to Vanderland.

"I'm afraid I'm going to have to shoot you," he said. "But first you're going to help us cart these walking-sticks out to the car. If you cause trouble I'll shoot you in a place you won't like."

Vanderland picked up an armload of walking-sticks and wondered just where he would like to be shot.

29

Parker was out in the DeSoto on the nightly round that he had recently started making. He could practically do it in his sleep.

But tonight was the night. He could feel it. He drove down by the old colonial village green, with the white-steepled church and with the Christmas tree lit up. He could see the College Inn looking cheerful decked in lights and snow.

Christmas music was still being blared out from the inn. "Good Kink Wennyslosh looked out on his feets uneven," sang the unmistakable voice of the famous blues singer Lomancee Phrolic; Betty, Bob Blanchard's college girl daughter, had selected the music.

Then Parker saw the station.

This was it at last. He had had a fifty-fifty chance of it working when he put Vanderland in there and it was working now. The door was opened and he saw Vanderland come out carrying the walking-sticks. Behind him, with a gun in his hand, was Summers. Also young Jake who loved Parker's daughter.

Parker had a gun in the glove compartment. He pulled it out. It was a .357 Magnum, big and heavy and very dangerous.

Well, Parker said to himself, you put Vanderland in there so the station would be an easy target.

That worked. Except now Vanderland has a gun shoved against his backbone. And you've got to do something.

He got out of the car and ducked down behind the door.

The gun's loaded, he said to himself. At least I think it is. He wondered if it still worked. He'd never fired it. An eerie slow motion took over. Boomer quite clearly could see Big Bad Bill's hate-filled eyes; the lids slowly closed then rose again.

"Stick 'em up," Parker said.

"Freeze," he said.

Summers didn't stick 'em up or freeze, he fired instead. There was a tremendous explosion and the Desoto got a hole in its door.

Parker stepped out of this cover behind the car door. Still he didn't fire, he only pointed the .357 Magnum in a lackadaisical way.

Then he ran towards Summers.

Vanderland was on the ground. Jake was running away. Parker wished he could run with him. It seemed the civilized thing to do.

Summers fired.

Not *the* leg again, Parker thought. No, it was the *other* leg.

He pushed himself into the air, waiting to feel a bullet in the chest or between the eyes.

He landed on Summers and brought him down.

He held the nozzle of the gun against Summer's head, but he could feel the strength dripping out of him along with the blood from his leg. Boomer when a ragged newspaper delivery boy had learned to punch when carrying the *Holford Evening Transcript* through the snobby streets of the rich end of North Holford where he was set upon by well-dressed bullies.

There's nothing else I can do, he thought. He drove his gunless left hand into Summer's face.

He must have a glass jaw, Parker said to himself as Big Bad Bill went out like most of the lights at the College Inn now did. "Merry Crimbo," Lomancee Phrolic managed to get in.

When I remember this, Parker thought, will the biggest thing be those lights going out?

Then he didn't think anymore. He was going down the old black slope, no longer little by little but all at once.

*

Parker was on his back in the station. Dr Phyllis Skypeck, like a too sexy looking guardian angel, was gazing down at him in a medical way.

Vanderland was standing behind her. He said, "You knew this was going to happen, didn't you, Boomer?"

"I figured you owed it to us after peddling drugs and trying to kill me."

Parker raised his head and looked around.

"Where's Summers?" he said.

"Locked up," Vanderland said. "I called Davy and Georgie while I stood guard over Big Bill. He started coming to so I tapped him a couple more times with that big gun of yours."

Davy was there too. "You used Vanderland as a patsy," he said to Parker.

"You were lucky," Georgie said. "He only had a .32."

"Not that lucky," Phyllis said. "But it was only a flesh wound."

Then Parker remembered Jake.

"Where the hell is he?"

"He got away," Davy said.

"Yeah," Georgie said, "he's long gone by now."

"We put out an APB. on him," Davy said, "and Captain Inez has got the State Troopers on to it."

"I think I saw him running to the College Inn," Parker said.

"He ain't there now," Davy said.

"Who says?"

"Everybody in the College Inn."

"Get me up," Parker said, "I want to go to the College Inn."

"I brought a wheelchair," Phyllis said. "You can't walk."

Parker lowered himself off the two desks where Vanderland in his dreams had been such a demon lover.

Phyllis guided Parker into the wheelchair.

"Georgie," Parker said, "You stay here and guard Summers."

The inn wasn't far away. Pushing Parker to it was a lot quicker than getting him and his wheelchair into a car and then out again.

"How's the DeSoto?" Parker asked.

"It's still got that hole in its door," Davy said.

"*The Red Badge of Courage*," Parker said.

"You got one in each leg," Phyllis said. "Also the shoulder."

"Yeah," Parker said. "Now maybe the Mayor won't fire me until next month."

They plowed the wheelchair through the snow and into the inn.

"What's this?" Bob Blanchard asked. "You're going to kill my business with all this crime."

"We've got to find Jake Summers," Parker said.

"He's not here."

"We told him that," Davy said.

There was an elevator and Parker went up in it.

"We already searched Jake's room," Davy said.

But Parker still lead them to the room. Jake's suitcase was there.

"Open it up," Parker said. It was packed.

"If it's packed, how come he didn't take it?"

"I dunno, Boomer. Maybe he was in too much of a hurry and forgot about it."

Parker looked about the room.

The windows were shut and locked.

Jake wasn't hiding in the shower with the curtain drawn.

"Look under the bed," Parker said.

"Boomer, that's kid's stuff."

"He's a kid isn't he?"

"OK," a voice said, "you got me."

Jake crawled out from under the bed. "I'm going to complain to Bob Blanchard about the maids not cleaning under the bed. Look at me." He was covered in dust. "I didn't kill no one. They were mostly all dead by the time I got there."

"Well, you took a shot at my daughter."

"How'd you know that was me?"

"You knew the dog and the dog knew you. And your uncle was very quick to say he had never seen the dog."

"Only that?" Jake said.

"Yes, if you criminals were actually intelligent we'd never catch you."

"I'm not a criminal. I'm only the nephew of a criminal."

"You better get your lawyer onto that."

They got back to the station.

"We've got to see Bill Summers," Parker said.

"He'll talk now," Davy said. "He's got nothing to lose."

"Where the hell's Georgie?" Parker said.

"Out in the back watching Summers in the cell," Davy said.

They went to the cells. Georgie wasn't there but Summers was, stretched out on the floor and as dead as they come with three bullet holes to prove it.

"Summers talking is strictly academic now, Davy," Parker said. "And what's more important, where's Georgie? Give him a call."

They reached Georgie. He was on the other side of the lake at Old Compton.

"Have you got a reason for being there?" Parker said.

"I did, but I don't no more. I got a call about a shooting over here, down the road from Whitey Gotton's sports shop. It was a hoax."

"Who made the call?"

"A woman. Or I think it was a woman or sort of sounded like one. Whatever, they said they was in trouble."

"What time was that?"

"Just after eleven o'clock."

"Jee-zuzz," Davy said when Parker told him the latest. "We're back to square one."

"I think we've got a way to go before we get that far," Parker said.

Georgie came back from Old Compton pleased with himself about driving over the ice on the lake.

He saw the ambulance parked outside the station.

"What's up?" he said.

"Another dead body," Parker said.

"Jee-zuzz, Georgie," Davy said. "Somebody tricked you into leaving Summers unguarded and then they walked in here and shot him."

"Golly," Georgie said.

"This has opened things up," Parker said. "Whoever's behind this is a tough sonofabitch to come in here and shoot Summers just in case he might talk."

"Who do we have left as suspects?" Davy said.

"Let's see," Parker said. "We've got the last remaining inmates up at Gledhill. Kindly Old Uncle Edward; that thin-lipped witch Maud Brewster and Mr and Mrs Hopkins; then there's Tom and Dick, the yardmen, there's also Vita and Margot. I can't think of anyone else."

"I can," Davy said, "there's that snooty English dame, your new girlfriend, Ottoline Smith, the ice-skating widow. We know she had one gun, maybe she had two."

30

Phyllis was watching over the body being taken away in the ambulance.

"How about you, Boomer?" she said.

"What do you mean?"

"What do I mean? You've been shot and you're in a wheelchair."

"I've got to get out of this thing."

He stood up.

"Hey," he said, "give me one of those walking-sticks."

It was only then that he realized they were gone.

*

Parker was back on two old walking-sticks, with no gold handles.

He was carrying a gun now, an ordinary police .38 revolver. He had given the .357 Magnum back to Davy. It hadn't been loaded.

He thought the .38 was better than that artillery piece. He was packing heat; because of the latest slaying he thought it the best thing to do. But he'd have to let go of one stick to take it out and fire it.

"Stay at home," Sue said.

Phyllis said the same thing. And Davy.

Jimmy Bichard was still in residence, following the adventures of that leaping, glowing hero Captain Elmo.

Jimmy's education was a cause now for Sue. She wanted to get him into a boarding school.

She said, "He's too clever to be in an ordinary school."

"You do what you think best," Parker said.

He started out the door on two sticks.

"What are you doing?" Sue said.

"I'm hobbling across the street to see if Tom and Dick, the former yardmen, have anything that looks like an alibi for last night."

Across the street at Mrs Wilson's the former Gledhill yardmen, Tom Slocum and Dick Gatz, had only each other for an alibi.

As well as looking like brothers they also looked guilty. Parker thought that Gatz, who had been a stick-up man in a very minor way in Cicero, outside Chicago, should have learned by now how to look innocent. It was something former stick-up men had to do because any time anyone was stuck up the police would come calling.

When Mrs Wilson finished fussing over Parker she said, "What time was this supposed to have happened?"

"We're certain about that, eleven, eleven-thirty."

"The boys were here, I know that for sure. I came to ask them if they wanted a hot drink and my grandfather clock in the hallway chimed the half hour."

But Parker wasn't finished with Tom and Dick.

"Who at Gledhill actually fired you?" he said.

"Edward," Tom said.

"That's right," Dick said. "Or maybe not Edward exactly."

"Yeah, not exactly," Tom said.

"Who exactly?"

"Didn't we tell you?"

"Tell me again."

"That tall thin school teacher," Tom said.

"She's not a school teacher," Dick said, "she's a college professor."

"What's the difference?" Tom said.

"I don't know," Dick said.

When Parker left Mrs Wilson's he telephoned Doris who used to be the Gledhill cook.

She told him how she had been in the kitchen at Gledhill and Maud had come in and told her she was fired.

"She came from Mr Edward," Doris said. "At least she said she did."

"You didn't think to ask him?"

"Not with all the deaths there had been in the house. I was glad to get out of there."

*

"I'm going out again," Parker said to Sue. "To Gledhill."

"How are you going to get there?"

"I'll drive."

"You can't drive. Not with that leg. You'll open the wound up. Come on, I'll take you."

She took hold of him and started leading him out.

Sue brushed the snow off the car. She wasn't used to the eccentricities of the DeSoto. She had trouble starting it. Getting it going forward was also difficult.

The East wind continued to blow. Then more snow started falling. The world was blanked out in whirling white. There was a silence too. Only the East wind whispered.

"Maybe we should turn back," Sue said.

"There's been murder. We've got to go on."

"We could skid off the road and be killed."

"Then the murders would be someone else's problem."

Jee-zuzz, Sue said to herself.

They reached Gledhill and it didn't seem so gloomy with a blizzard blocking Parker's view.

He would have liked to tell Sue to stay in the car but it was too cold for that. She came to the house with him.

They stood there stamping their feet. Sue waved her arms about to keep warm. She was wearing a thick Norwegian ski sweater, blue with big snowflakes and a deer. Her hair suddenly hung down over the left side of her face. She looked like a 1940s film star. Parker couldn't remember the star's name.

Parker wasn't looking forward to getting the standard Maud greeting when she opened the door. But when it was answered it wasn't Maud. It was Kindly Old Uncle Edward.

"There's a fire again in the library," he said. "I can't imagine what Maud was thinking when she stopped doing that. I lit the fire myself. Luckily there was enough chopped wood stacked up in the yard. Besides, I turned on the central heating. Why did she turn that off? She told me it was broken. Why should she say that?"

"Why don't you ask her?" Sue said.

"I can't. She'd get angry. You've seen her. You know what she's like."

"Good Lord," Sue said, "she's always angry. Where did you find her?"

STANLEY REYNOLDS

"At Abigail Jefferson. She instructs the ladies in what's called Gracious Living. I thought that would include cooking, but apparently it doesn't."

"I suspect they think they'll have cooks – or chefs," Sue said.

"Who lives like that anymore?" the Kindly Old Uncle said, making a gesture with his hands.

"Well," Sue said, "you do."

"Only when I am staying with Andrew."

Veronica Lake, Parker thought, that was the name of the actress with the hair curving down one side of her face. She was known as The Look. Before Parker's TV set broke he'd seen *I Married a Witch*, with Veronica Lake.

Parker didn't mind Sue taking over. He could study Edward better that way.

He was certainly a jolly old soul. There was still the Christmas spirit alive in Gledhill when he was standing there being kindly in front of the big, tastefully decorated Christmas tree in the hallway. The top of it, with a star, reached all the way up the stairs. You expected Santa Claus to come in and ask if he had forgot to give them everything they asked for.

Parker had never found out what Edward had done for a living. Could he have been an actor, was all this kindly uncle put on?

He asked him. Edward said, "Do you think I could have been an actor? I was in the Hasty Pudding Theatricals. I played a very minor part in one show."

Parker thought that the college show might have been enough training for Edward to carry off the Kindly Old Uncle performance.

2 1 2

The front door opened and Davy came in with a blast of cold air.

"I thought I should ought to give you a hand, Boomer."

He saw the bulge of the .38 in the inside pocket of Parker's much abused tweed jacket.

"I see you're carrying that roscoe," he said.

Parker turned to Sue. "Find yourself a book to read and sit by the fire in the library," he said.

There was much loud knocking on the front door. It swung open.

Sue didn't go to the library. She stood awaiting the latest entertainment.

"Oh, brother," Davy said.

The gentlemen of the press were there, led by Johnny Peru of the *New York Daily Jolt* and Vince Vanilla of the *Boston Evening Lightning*.

"This is a helluva story, Chief," Peru said.

"Yeah," Vanilla said.

Peru looked at Sue and said, "Is this still your daughter, Chief?"

"Yes," Parker said, "all day long."

"Anything you want to call her is OK by me," Vanilla said. He looked like he was going to wink.

"With Summers shot full of holes," Peru said, "it shows there's no honor among gunmen. By the way, Boomer, do you know you got a Chicago hitman here?"

"Dick Gatz, a stick-up guy," Vanilla said.

"He's got an alibi," Sue said.

"Alibi Gatz," Peru said, "such names are made for tabloid headlines."

"Gatz was sixteen years old," Parker said, "and it was a replica gun and he got a slap on the wrist and that was it."

"Was that it?" Peru said.

"That was it," Parker said.

"Now clear out," Davy said. "This is a murder scene."

They backed out the door.

"Now," Davy said, "we can round up the usual suspects."

31

Spectral Maud was obviously the first one to interview.

Davy was in such a hurry to have at her that he blundered into the study where she was and came close to knocking her over.

"You got an alibi?" he asked. "They all got alibis. Phoney alibis. I'll bet yours is pretty phoney too. Try it out on me and I'll let you know."

Maud, in a lime green tweed coat and skirt, with a jasper blouse, pulled herself upright even more than nature had intended. She looked a deadly look down her high bridged nose.

"Are you drunk?" Maud said. "Or have you been over indulging in stupidity?"

Parker didn't go with Davy to interview Maud. He stood silently in the front hall thinking about the father of Jack Smith broken down with grief. There was Donald Billings' relatives too, and although he hadn't met them yet the mothers and fathers of the others. Even Bruce Dane had Rosie, the waitress from Sam's Spaghetti House, to weep for him. There must be someone also in the vast Western regions of Mimi of the Movies' past who would think of her gone mad thousands of miles away on the other side of the country. Those were "the accessories of death which are in a sense more memorable than death itself," the literary Boomer thought.

Parker turned away from these sad thoughts and went into the study to learn what Maud had to say.

The study had a walnut desk with a leather covered chair behind it, both desk and chair were big and expensive looking.

Maud and Davy were seated in uncomfortable looking ladder back chairs on opposite sides of the room. They looked like chess players who had forgotten the board and the pieces.

Davy said, "Something's very wrong here." He looked at Maud and said, "You tell Boomer."

"Who's Boomer?"

"Boomer's Boomer."

"That's me," Parker said.

Davy read from his notebook, "Miss Maud Brewster of Abigail Jefferson College claims she never said nothing to no one."

"Mr Daniels," Maud said, "are you in control of this person of abnormally weak intellect?"

"She claims she didn't do nothing," Davy said.

"Good God," Maud said, "I didn't fire Doris, the cook, or those two oafs, Tom Slocum and Dick Gatz."

"Who did?"

"I don't know. It would have to have been Edward. It could be no one else."

She came as near to shaking with rage as a superior well-bred woman full of Gracious Living could come.

Davy said, "Are you sure you're telling us Old Edward didn't send you to sack no one?"

"Good Lord, how many times must I say it?" She sighed, turning her knife-thin face's vermillion nose to the left and right, seeking something in the room to throw and break.

They left Maud alone and went to find Edward.

He was sitting by a fire in an old-fashioned room in what should be the West Wing. He had a book held up close to his eyes even though he was wearing his half-moon spectacles. He looked like an illustration of Mr Bennett in *Pride and Prejudice*.

Parker told Edward what Maud said.

"This is extraordinary," Edward chuckled in kindly Old Uncle Edward fashion. "What could have gotten into her? I never sent her to sack Doris or Tom and Dick, the yardmen."

"Why do you think they left?"

"I assumed they quit."

"They say they were sacked by Miss Brewster, acting for you."

"They weren't. Is Maud having a joke? I'd never dismiss anyone at Christmas time. I shouldn't speak ill of the dead, but that is more in my late brother Andrew's style."

They left the performance. Davy said, "One of them's lying."

Maud appeared. There was something theatrical about her too.

Parker told her what Edward said. She was shocked. "I'm not remaining here a moment longer," she said.

"You ain't gonna leave no town?" Davy said.

"No, I ain't gonna. I'm going back to Abigail Jefferson."

Parker found Jane Hopkins in the kitchen. He asked where she was at the time of Bill Summers' murder.

"Eleven o'clock or eleven-thirty? I was upstairs in bed."

"Where was Mr Hopkins? Was he with you?"

"No, he wasn't. I was alone. I don't know where he was. He told me but I forget what he said."

"What time did he come in?"

"I didn't pay much attention. Maybe two o'clock in the morning? I was fast asleep."

"Maybe he's our man," Davy said. He was eating a Maryland chocolate chip cookie that Jane had baked. "It smells real good in this kitchen," he added.

Jane was busy. She looked happy even if she was being treated like a prime suspect.

"Who gave you the cook's job?" Parker said.

"No one. I just assumed it. We had to eat."

When they left her in the kitchen Davy said, "Stephen Hopkins sure looks a sure thing. His wife's landed him in it."

Stephen was in the billiard room. Not playing but smoking.

"I've got to stop this," he said. "I had stock in a cigarette company so I kept it up. But the stock's useless. I'm going to stop."

Davy said, "Where did you get the money for this restaurant you're gonna open in Philly?"

"I had it."

"Or you will after selling them gold walking-sticks," Davy said.

"What time did you come home last night?" Parker said.

"I never went out. I was down here trying not to smoke."

"What time did you go to bed?"

"I don't know. Not late."

"Will your wife confirm that?"

"She can't. She wasn't there. Whatever time it was I fell right asleep dreaming of being in a tobacco trance until I woke up and had to have a cigarette."

"She was there in the morning?"

"No. I suppose she was already in the kitchen."

When they left him Davy said:

"What's going on, Boomer? First she drops him in it and then he does it to her."

*

Vita was in her room looking out of the window.

"I don't seem to get bored looking at it snowing," she said. "It's not like rain. I don't want to look at rain. Except in April when it lets you know that something beautiful is about to happen."

"Breeding lilacs out of the dead land," Parker said.

Vita smiled; a little raising of the lips in recognition.

Jee-zuzz, Davy said to himself, the Mayor gotta hear about them whimsicalities.

"Where was you at eleven-thirty last night?" Davy said.

"In here."

"What was you doing?"

"Drinking. I do little else."

"So youse told me when your sister ran away from them ghosts."

"So I'm telling youse again."

There was a bottle of wine along with a long stemmed glass on the bedside table.

She filled the glass. It was a very big glass.

"This way," she said, "I keep the number of glasses down."

219

They got nothing more out of her.

"Let's go see the redhead sister, Margot, at Coot Williams' place," Parker said.

He told Sue she should take the DeSoto home and he went, bent supporting himself on the walking-sticks, to the police car.

Davy said, "When you going to see that Ottoline dame, Boomer? You can't let her off no hook."

"After Margot and Coot. Maybe Coot will give you an autographed baseball."

"I already got one."

"Maybe this time he'll sign it Lou Gehrig, maybe even Babe Ruth."

The driving was still bad going.

"What the hell are you going to do with a cripple if the car gets stuck?" Parker said.

Davy didn't answer. It was, Parker thought, a rhetorical question.

Parker said, "When old Mrs Wilson heard the half hour chime on her grandfather clock why didn't she look at her wristwatch?"

This time it wasn't rhetorical.

"Why should she?" Davy said.

"Because everyone would," Parker said.

*

Coot Williams had cleared the snow off the path leading to the front door.

Parker wondered if love was still in bloom inside.

Margot, haunted no longer by Gledhill ghosts, was glowing. She looked like an advertisement, but what for Parker didn't know. Something healthy.

There was a nice smell coming from the kitchen.

"It's a fish Coot got out of a hole in the ice on the lake," she said.

"Where was you last night at some time like eleven-thirty?" Davy said.

"Sit down, Chief Daniels," Margot said, "before you fall down."

She attempted to help Parker into a chair.

"I'm all right," Parker said.

Margot turned to Davy and said:

"Eleven-thirty? I was in bed."

"You got confirmation for that?"

"Yes, Coot."

"Anyone else?"

She looked at Davy with one of those Maud Brewster looks that questioned his intellect.

Davy recognized it.

"Oh, yeah," he said, "sorry. Coot and youse is like honeymooners now, you don't want no witnesses. Am I right?"

"Youse ain't wrong," Margot said.

Davy gazed at the room as if he might see the gold walking-sticks piled up in a corner.

Coot, a tall lean figure in a crimson and Prussian blue lumberjacket, came in with an armload of chestnut brown logs and carefully placed them in a stack by the open fire – ruby flames with white smoke.

Davy looked at him as if Coot were coming in to bat in the top half of the ninth inning when only a home run would save the day for the Yankees.

Not for the first time Parker wished he could love something as much as Davy loved baseball.

Davy wasn't going to dare to ask him, so Parker did.

"Where were you at eleven-thirty last night, Coot?"

"Right here, upstairs."

Parker pulled himself out of the chair.

I've got to get rid of these sticks, he thought. I'm not a victim. I'm the guy who protects the victims.

They got in the car and managed to get through the snow. Parker thought about crime. Davy was still thinking of baseball.

"A lot of people don't know this, Boomer," Davy said, "but I had a try out as a catcher for Brownville in the North Atlantic League."

"Did you?"

"I did."

Parker had heard it before. Too many times to keep count.

32

Skaters were out on the ice at the Lake House, the wind blew flurries around them, and it was a North East wind but they didn't notice. It was a frozen Eden. But Ottoline was not among the gaily colored skaters.

They went up the steps to the porch of the hotel behind them, if they had turned, the ice was indistinguishable from the sky; except for the blue and red and green swooping and twirling figures. The porch was covered in glass during the winter. In the summer it would have screens to let the air in and keep the insects out.

Parker and Davy were so familiar with the Lake House that they stepped into the lobby as if it were something they owned.

At the bar were two long legs attached to an English accent.

They weren't going to distract Davy from his duty.

"Where was you …"

He paused, remembering his grammar.

"Where was youse at last night at eleven-thirty?" he said.

"I went out for a midnight stroll and I happened to see Bill Summers so I killed him."

"How'd you know about Summers being murdered?"

"Everybody knows about it. This is a small town no matter how many big city cops are in it."

"Smart ass remarks don't gonna to get youse nowhere."

"I was here."

"Who was behind the bar?"

"Gus was."

"Gus who?"

"I don't know Gus who."

"I know Gus. Gus is Gus Schmidt."

"From where?" Ottoline said.

"From here. Say, are you being funny?"

"Only trying to be."

"Well, try better or stop doing it. Gus ain't working now on account of he was working last night. He'll know if you was here."

"Give him a call," Parker said.

"I think I will."

Barry was behind the bar.

"You know where Gus is today?" Davy asked him.

"At home I suppose."

"You suppose? You mean you don't know?"

"Why should I know?"

"I'll call him, I'll call Gus."

"Here's his number," Barry said.

"Whose number?"

"Gus's number."

"Do you want a drink?" Ottoline said to Parker while Davy was making the call.

"I think I need one," Parker said.

He had a beer. He wondered if he should be suspicious. Just who was Ottoline Smith? A pair of legs and a blonde head of hair, also blue beamers, didn't do anything but make her look innocent.

"He was here," Davy said when he came back. "Gus was here and she was here too with Gus. I guess you got away with it this time. But don't leave town."

"I won't be leaving town. At least I hope I won't be. I'm putting in for a job."

"Where?"

"Right here," she said.

"Where right here?"

"At Abigail Jefferson," she said to Parker. "Maud Brewster wants to go to Boston. She says she might be safe on Beacon Hill."

"Safe from what?"

"People like us. In the meantime she said she was going to suggest they take me on as an art teacher for the rest of the school year."

"Will you have to teach Gracious Living?" Parker said.

"I guess I'm going to be forced to."

They drove up the hill that ran from the Lake House to the tall steepled white-painted church and the snow covered village green.

"I'd love it to be that Ottoline broad," Davy said.

Davy parked in front of the station. Parker got out. There was still pain in his left leg. There was also pain in his right leg. Maybe next time I can get shot in an arm, he thought. Then he was reminded of the pain in his shoulder.

Davy was thinking in a sporting metaphor.

"We need a slam dunk right about now, Boomer," he said.

Georgie was in the station. He held the phone up to Parker as they came in.

"It's Margot Cuncliffe. You know, the redhead in the green drawers. She says she's thought of something you ought to know."

Parker sat down letting his sticks fall on the floor. He took the phone from Georgie.

"Chief Parker," she said, "I've just remembered something you should know. My brain has been clogged up with coke. But I'm all right now. My nose has almost stopped running and my brain is working again, partly."

"I'm glad to hear that."

"And maybe you'll be glad to hear this. That wasn't ghosts I heard at Gledhill. I guess you knew that. What I saw were two men. Two real live men."

"Do they have real live names?"

"I didn't know their names then, but I do now. I described them and Coot told me. Tom Slocum and Dick Gatz."

"I know where they are," Parker said. He paused for a moment and then he said, "Don't tell anyone about this. It wouldn't be safe. I'll get a statement from you later."

"What was that, Boomer?" Davy said. "Was that anything?"

"I think it might be the slam dunk we've been looking for."

He told Davy what Margot Cuncliffe said.

"That's the stuff," Davy said. "That's straight down the middle."

*

Old Mrs Wilson's house looked empty as Davy pulled up.

Sue must have heard the car because she stepped out on the porch of Parker's house.

"Are you coming in, Dad?"

"Not yet," Parker said. "In a little while."

Mrs Wilson answered the door. She was pleased to see them.

"How's your leg, Parker? I should say legs. And, of course, the rest of you."

She had been a friendly nurse when she worked at the Holford City Hospital. The patients loved her.

"Mrs Wilson," Parker said, "when you heard your grandfather clock chime at eleven-thirty did you look at your wristwatch?"

"I did but it wasn't there. I must have taken it off and left it somewhere. I found it the next day. It had got under the bed in one of the spare rooms."

"Who's using that room?"

"Mr Gatz. It must have fallen off my wrist when I was making the bed." She glanced down at her watch. "The strap seems perfectly all right now," she said.

"Where's Gatz? And Tom Slocum?"

"They're not here, they went out."

"May I take a look at their rooms?"

Parker went into Gatz's room and Davy went to Slocum's. Their clothes weren't there. Nothing was there.

Parker and Davy left Mrs Wilson's.

Sue came out on the porch again.

"Did you see Tom and Dick leaving here?" Parker asked, calling to her from across the road.

"I saw them," a voice behind Sue said.

"Jee-zuzz," Davy said, "it's the Wilson kid."

The Wilson kid came down the porch stairs. He said:

"I was coming over here to bring a couple of comic books for Jimmy and I seen Tom driving off in his car and Dick driving off in that old pick-up of his."

"Driving where?"

"I don't know exactly but they headed into where all them college buildings is at."

"Are you coming in, Dad?" Sue called, standing on the snowy porch with her hair falling over one eye and her arms crossed to keep warm.

"I'd like to but I haven't got the time."

He got into the car. Davy drove.

The streets were icy. It was difficult driving. Once they swung around almost as if they going back to where they'd come from.

Davy took his right hand off the wheel and moved his gun up and down in its holster as if he might have to beat someone to the draw.

"What are you gonna do, Boomer?"

Parker said he'd have to wait and see.

Davy said:

"I got a shotgun in the trunk of this car. You could use it as a walking-stick and then if you have to you could whip it up and waste any bastard who was handy."

"That would make my holiday season," Parker said.

"You bet," Davy said. Parker looked at him. Davy's eyes had a bright light in them and his mouth was set in a determined little grin. "I hope that Wilson kid was right," Davy said.

33

The Wilson kid was. They saw the pick-up truck parked outside an Abigail Jefferson building.

"It's the art department," Parker said.

Turning right off the main road that carried cars, horsemen, bicyclists and pedestrians through North Holford to the woods, the big college buildings took visitors by surprise. Built to mimic English manors, French chateaux or even one extraordinary parody of Italian Risorgimento, they were covered in ivy. Sometimes they were called "our ancient ivy halls of learning" – the art department was housed in one of these.

"Do you see who I see?" Davy said.

It was Ottoline. She was in a ground floor room. Parker could see her standing in front of the window, with her blue eyes like the blue of a cerulean sky.

They got out of the car. Parker managed to get ahead of Davy. He said, "Keep behind me, and don't fire that gun. And if you must shoot someone make sure it's me. The citizens must be protected."

"What's that?" Davy said. "Someone's talking."

They heard a voice. It said, "Hi! this is Pip Pipgrass. Do you oldtimers remember this one? It's Millie singing about her boy lollipop who makes her heart go hippity hop."

Millie started singing. Parker thought as background music for a shootout Pip Pipgrass could play something less cheerful.

"They're doing something and they don't want us to hear," Davy said.

Parker moved slowly towards the sound of the radio.

Pip Pipgrass cut Millie off.

"Here's some bad news for you sports fans," he said. "It looks like the Pats and Jets won't be playing on account of the blizzard."

Parker heard Davy swear.

"What are we gonna do with you?" someone said. The voice wasn't Pip Pipgrass's.

"We gotta start getting this stuff out of here," another voice said. "Then we can see what we gotta do."

Parker knew those voices. Tom Slocum and Dick Gatz were in there.

"That English Ottoline babe's in there," Davy whispered in Parker's ear. "If I shoot is it OK if I have to shoot her?"

"There's somebody out there," Dick Gatz suddenly said. "I just heard them."

"There ain't nobody there," Tom Slocum said.

"I heard them."

"You're getting the jitters."

"Sure I got the jitters. Don't you?"

"Yeah, with all this gold we gotta sneak out of here."

"Well, we sneaked it out of Old Man Burgess's place to be hid here. We can sneak it out of here."

"What do you think we got here?"

"Millions."

"No more yardmen for us."

"I didn't mind being a yardman."

"Neither did I."

"Trouble is there's been them murders!"

"We didn't make no guy dead."

"But we know who did. That's the trouble."

"Yeah, that's the trouble."

"Big trouble."

All this time the radio kept playing music and when it wasn't Pip Pipgrass was telling what bargains there were in various local stores. Inspite of Brucie Dane having been murdered his supermarkets were still offering specials.

Parker was thinking that if Tom and Dick didn't kill anyone then who did kill Dane and Summers?

"We're going to get a big pay off," Tom Slocum said.

"If they don't kill us."

"Why should they do that?"

"They killed Summers didn't they."

"They thought he might talk. They can't kill us, we know too much."

"That'll do it."

"I'd like to see them try. I'll ice them all real good. Then it will all be ours."

"But how could we get rid of it? Gold ain't something no couple of ordinary guys can sell to no one."

"That's true."

"Goddamn right it is."

"What the hell is this thing in aid of?" Dick Gatz suddenly asked.

"It's Aztec," a woman said.

Parker knew the voice. It was Ottoline.

Davy nudged him and smiled.

"What's Aztec," Gatz said.

"They ruled Mexico until the Spanish came."

"But what did they do with this thing?"

"It's a Winged Serpent, one of their gods."

"It's their God?"

"Just one of them."

"It's sick. It sure looks sick," Slocum ssaid.

"It ain't Santa Claus," Gatz said.

Parker thought they had been standing outside long enough. They knew what was going on and who was doing it. He had hoped to hear them mention the brains behind it, but they didn't and he felt he couldn't wait.

He put one stick on the floor and took out the .38. He was standing OK on one stick, but would he be able to walk?

He paused. There were footsteps entering from an adjoining room.

A new voice spoke.

"Why did you come here?" it said.

Parker and Davy knew that voice. It was Maud Brewster.

"I wanted to see where everything was," Ottoline said.

"And you saw too much of it," Maud said. "In a world run as it should be, one of these morons would have killed you. But I'm going to have to do it."

"Not while we're here seeing it," Tom said.

"Close your eyes then."

Parker opened the door and fell into the room. He was lucky. Maud fired and it missed him because he was already on the floor.

"Freeze," Davy said, but she was already out of the door on the other side of the room.

Ottoline tried to help Parker stand up. She couldn't do it.

Tom and Dick helped.

"That don't win you no points," Davy told them. "Who else is in this? Are you in it?" he asked Ottoline.

"It's obvious that she isn't," Parker said. "Maud was going to shoot her."

"They shot Bill Summers and he was one of their pals."

"We didn't shoot no one," Tom Slocum said.

"I was a stick-up guy in Cicero, outside Chicago, but I wasn't no good at it," Dick said. "I had a toy gun."

"Boomer," Davy said, "don't tell me you're going to let these guys go."

Tom laughed.

"It ain't funny," Davy said, "he let Bob Vanderland go."

"Can we join the police too?" Tom said.

"Cut the comedy," Davy said.

"Parker," Ottoline said, "may I go back to the Lake House?"

"You're coming with us, babe," Davy said. "We gotta lock you up until everything's jake."

"There's no need to do that. She can drive me," Parker said.

"Where will we go then, Boomer?" Davy said.

"We'll go after Maud."

"And where's she?"

"At Gledhill."

Davy took Tom and Dick to the police station to lock them up. Ottoline drove Parker in Tom's pick-up truck.

They were driving by the turn off to Parker's street.

"Turn here," Parker said.

His leg was feeling better now. Or maybe it was because he had something to do. Anyway he got out of the pick-up truck and up the icy porch steps to his house.

"What's going on?" Sue said. "I was told there was shooting."

"Who told you that?"

"Davy, I called the station."

"I want you to do something for me."

Sue looked at Ottoline to see if he wanted to take her in. Ottoline didn't look a charity case.

"See if you can get something on the Internet for me," Parker said.

"I could do it," Jimmy said.

"I'll do it," Sue said. "What is it?"

"I want to know where you sell gold. I should have looked this up ages ago."

Sue sat down in front of her computer.

"Look at this," she said.

There was a testimonial from a customer, Herb F. of Baltimore. He was happy. The people Herb F. was happy about bought gold and gold jewelery. They paid Top-Dollar Deals For Your Gold.

"And look at this," she said.

There was a name there that he recognized.

"I should have known," he said.

Ottoline had seen what the Internet revealed.

She drove the pick-up to Gledhill and Parker did his thinking aloud.

"They can probably sell gold bars and we couldn't trace them. But gold jewelry is different. It can be traced. At least it can for a while, but let enough time go by and it would be safe to sell."

The weather had changed. The snow was melting. Snow fell off the roof of Gledhill. But this weather change didn't bring a good day. The mountain and the fields leading up to it were hidden behind a heavy veil of fog. The end of the world once more. There was an eerie stillness. No wind stirred the dense gray fog. Life was at a standstill.

Davy's car followed the pick-up to the front door.

Parker filled him in on what the Internet had disclosed.

"The trouble is," Parker said, "he wasn't here when people were being killed."

The front door was locked. They knocked.

"Well," Davy said, "at least it won't be that spooky Maud broad."

"Unless she answers the door with her pistol drawn."

Ottoline was standing behind them.

"You gonna keep her with us, Boomer?" Davy said.

"She can sit by the open fire in the library and think she's having an old-fashioned New England Christmas."

They heard footsteps coming across the hall to the front door.

"Well, here we go," Parker said. He didn't sound optimistic. He wasn't about to break into song.

"'Death was in that house and Hell Yawned before it,'" Ottoline said, quoting Virginia Woolf.

Then she remembered murder most foul and became less literary.

34

A drowsy calm had descended on gloomy Gledhill. It was peaceful, even pleasant in a few corners of a few rooms. One room was even happy. This was the kitchen where Jane Hopkins, the formerly unhappy housewife of Philadelphia, was stirring something in a saucepan. "Soup," she sang, "so rich and green waiting in a hot tureen!"

She was not the only busy inmate. At this time the characters assembled at Gledhill were performing various tasks.

While Jane Hopkins was stirring, Stephen Hopkins was putting on an apron in order to help her and he was wondering if it was more *macho* if he didn't tie the apron strings. He decided it was and lit a cigarette to celebrate the unfastened apron before he remembered he was engrossed in a fierce battle to give up this fleeting, and deadly and blissful pursuit.

Meanwhile in the morning-room Captain Inez Bodegus of the State Police was studying herself in a looking-glass. She wondered if she would ever be pursued by men other than Sergeant O'Brien.

Johnny Peru of the *New York Daily Jolt* was in the Gledhill living-room going through the bar in the corner looking for a bottle which had something written in American on it.

Vince Vanilla of the *Boston Evening Lighting* was lounging on the other side of the room drinking whatever beer it was that was making Milwaukee famous that week. He was wondering if Johnny Peru had got himself a story that was being kept from him.

Meanwhile in an obscure part of the house Hapless Jones of the *Holford Evening Transcript* had just stumbled upon a stack of drink. Bottles of claret and gin and one of Vermouth had been put under a sofa.

Hapless knew big time reporters Peru and Vanilla were seeking drink. He thought he should tell them about this cache. But he was reading a detective story and he was almost at the end. He lounged back on the sofa and started to read. Rosilita, the showgirl from the Rancho Descansada, was going to spill the beans. Rosilita told whodunnit. It was Bugs Malloy. Hapless knew it all the time.

Then he thought he should show this mysterious cache of bottles to Parker Daniels.

*

Vita Cuncliffe was in her room walking back and forth in front of the colonial four poster. She had happy thoughts of the future..

Maud Brewster was in the garden-room hiding behind an orange tree wondering how she could flee with her pockets full of gold. The bad luck walking-sticks were in the house but how could she get away with them? The 1929 Cadillac, with its golden speaking-tube, flower vase, headlights, hub caps and numerous parts of engine, was in the garage ready to go but she had to get to it.

That international man of business Earl P. Vanderland was in the library wondering who had time to read

books, or even book. High finance was out there waiting
for him and he must get to it.

Meanwhile Kindly Old Uncle Edward was crossing
the front hall to answer the ringing and knocking
at the door. He opened it and gave Parker, Davy and
Ottoline such a bright beaming smile that you would
have thought no one had ever uttered a cross word in
Gledhill, let alone decorated the place with corpses.

He was so much a perfect picture of innocence that
Parker thought he must be guilty of something.

There was an urgent shuffle of hurrying feet; Parker
looked up and saw Hapless coming down the stairs by
the big all dolled-up Christmas tree. He looked like a
Tiny Tim version of a crime reporter.

"What the hell are you up to, buster?" Davy said.
"You look like them cats what got the cream."

"It's Boomer not you I wanna tell something,"
Hapless said.

He took Parker to see the mystery cache. "It's a
strange place to stash them," Hapless said looking at
the bottles.

"I've been looking for something like this. Don't
handle them. They may have finger-prints that'll prove
interesting."

Parker returned to the front hall. He told Davy
where the bottles were.

"Check them for prints," he said. They had everyone's
finger prints with which to compare them.

"Chief Daniels," Uncle Edward said, "those
walking-sticks have shown up again. I found them
in the garden-room. Do you want a couple? They're
better looking than those old rustic-looking ones
of yours."

He waved a hand at the sticks now back in the elephant foot stand in the corner. "I put them back this morning," he said.

"I think I better take a look at the garden-room," Parker said, "you stay here, Ottoline."

Ottoline stood there looking like an out of work extra.

Parker went to the back of the house to the garden-room. He was trying to walk with only one stick. He had the second stick hooked over his left arm just in case.

The .38 was in his pocket. It made him feel uncomfortable.

You're stuck with this, he told himself as he limped into the garden-room where he saw someone hiding behind the orange tree and whoever it was saw him.

She had taken a shot at him before and she took another shot at him now.

She missed but Parker was on the floor again; Maud was unlucky the way Parker fell down every time she tried to shoot him. The lime tweed and jasper bloused Maud started to flee. A dramatic looking figure, tall and thin, with a sinister face, all nose and eyes. She looked like one of the cartoon villains Captain Elmo fought.

Parker turned the stick in his right hand around and hooked one of Maud's beige stocking legs. She went face down and her pistol went off again followed by the sound of breaking glass.

There was then the sound of running feet and Davy came in followed by Ottoline and Uncle Edward.

"Are you dead, Boomer?" Davy asked looking at the sprawled Parker.

"He's not dead is he?" Ottoline said.

"He can't be dead," Uncle Edward said. "We can't have another one. It isn't even Twelfth Night yet."

Davy sat on Maud. He had her Gluck gun in his hand.

"I was going to get one of these," he said to her, "but I thought it had too much of a kickback to hit anything."

"Don't I know it?" she said. "Just look at me, you moron."

"You'll know better next time," Davy said. "Not that there's gonna be no next time. If I had my way you'd be sitting on Old Sparkie, but you'll at least get life."

"Who's in it with you?" Parker said. No longer sprawled he was sitting on the floor. "Get off her, Davy," he said. "And help me up. What about the finger-prints on the bottles."

"There weren't none."

"I thought so," Parker said, "but we don't have to let everybody know that. Know what I mean?"

"I sure do, I think," Davy said.

Georgie Stover appeared. He helped Parker to his feet.

"Who's minding the store?" Parker asked.

"Vanderland," Georgie said. "I figured it was OK and you might need help here."

"There's someone we're looking for," Parker said.

He went upstairs pulling himself on the banister with one hand and pushing upward with a stick in the other hand. Johnny Peru and Vince Vanilla were waiting for him at the top of the stairs.

Parker opened the door of Vita Cuncliffe's bedroom and saw her sitting there looking like a front cover of *Vogue.*

"You boys stay out here," Parker told Peru and Vanilla.

He walked in.

Vita looked at Parker. She didn't smile but why should she?

She was dressed in black. Black legs, black skirt and black sweater.

Parker looked and he wondered what he should be seeing. Then he saw it.

There was a gold brooch pinned on the sweater. There was other jewellery too. All gold.

"You certainly are a real woman," he said, "wearing jewellery no matter how dangerous it is to wear it."

"This is my own," she said.

"It can be traced. You should have thought of that. And we found your prints on a bottle."

"That's a lie," she said and then she realized she had let him know that she knew about the bottles.

Davy came in.

"What about it?" Parker said.

"What about what?"

"About that thumb print on that bottle."

"Oh, yeah, it's her print," Davy said.

"And look at her. Does she look like she has a hangover? Or ever had one?"

"That's right," Davy said, "when I interviewed her and she said how drunk she'd got the night before I thought there was something wrong."

Davy went to get the reporters out of the way.

"Do you actually drink?" Parker said to Vita.

She didn't say anything. She simply aimed her dangerous ice cold blue eyes at him.

Parker said, "You used it as an excuse. Your sister was passed out on drugs and you were out helping Tom Slocum and Dick Gatz move gold out of here."

"Who sez?"

"Tom and Dick sez. We've also got Maud. She'll start talking when her lawyer does some plea bargaining and she wants the law to go easy on her."

"You disgusting hick," Vita said.

She leaped out of the chair and reached out for something on the dressing table.

Too late Parker saw what it was. She had a bejewelled gold handled dagger. The eyes were like Andrew's had been when he was pretending to be one of the less sociable reptiles.

There was a struggle like a primitive dance, one dancer with flashing dagger and the other armed with two walking-sticks, one stick to hold him upright and the other to poke at the mad Vita. He poked it into her, pinning her to the wall.

She struck at him with the dagger, slashing it back and forth. Her arm wasn't long enough.

"You're not going to limp out of here," she said. "You're not even going to be able to crawl."

She made a special effort. Her arm was still too short.

Parker hit her wrist. The dagger fell to the floor.

"Bastard," she said. She was a tough bimbo all right. It must have come natural, Parker thought, they didn't teach tough bimbo at Bryn Mawr.

Parker shouted, "Come in boys, I've got something for you."

Peru and Vanilla and Hapless came into the room.

Parker said, "She's probably the one who went to the station and killed Bill Summers. It was either her or Maud Brewster. There's one more still to go," he added.

"Who's that?" Peru said.

"Earl P. Vanderland."

Earl P. was the man who bought gold. The one Herb F. of Baltimore endorsed in capital letters.

"Who'd he croak?" Peru asked.

"Bruce Dane."

"But Earl P. had an alibi."

"From Rosie, the waitress at Sam's Spaghetti House. I don't think that will hold up. She phoned him at the number he had left for her. He kept her talking until he reached the station and Bob Vanderland could talk to her."

Maud and Vita were cuffed and Captin Inez was carting these lethal ladies off to the County jail.

The fog was still thick. The mountain was only a rumor where they were standing at Gledhill's front door.

"I sincerely hope this is the end," Uncle Edward said. "If they wanted gold so much I would have given it to them," he added, breaking a record for kindness.

"Have you seen Earl P. Vanderland?" Parker asked.

"He's not here," Uncle Edward said. "He left a few minutes ago. But he can't have anything to do with this. He's got half of all the money in the world."

"He wants the other half," Parker said. "What get away car did Earl P. use?"

The garage doors were open.

Parker could see the 1929 Cadillac was no longer there.

"He's gone," Parker told Davy. "In the Golden Chariot."

They were standing by the front door in the well-iced fog looking a little lost without Earl P. in handcuffs.

"Where'd he go?" Davy said.

"Either to Mexico or Canada," Park said. "Just like in the movies."

From inside the house they heard a radio playing a Christmas carol. "God rest ye merry gentlemen," a choir sang, "let nothing you dismay …"

35

Kindly Old Uncle Edward had a Twelfth Night party. Hardly anyone knew exactly what Twelfth Night was when it wasn't Shakespeare but the idea that someone might be murdered brought out all North Holford, even Peg Bichard, Jimmy's mother; Rosie the waitress from Sam's; and Sam himself.

Sue wasn't there. She was back in Boston. She was better off there, Parker thought. He'd see her, and Daisy, in the summer.

Phyllis was looking attractive and kept getting as up close and personal with Parker as she could. It was the holiday spirit.

Coot Williams looked in. Margot was visiting Vita in the County jail.

Kindly Old Uncle Edward told Peg that he'd pay for Jimmy's education. Then he told Ottaline that she should live at Gledhill rather than some inferior place that Abigail Jefferson College would put her in. Ottaline asked Parker to call her Ottaline. He didn't tell her to call him Boomer.

Old Uncle Edward thought of that gray thing that looked back at him from the not too distant future. Give them all money, he said to himself. It was the best thing he could think of.

*

A week later Parker was sitting with Davy as cozy as Holmes and Dr Watson in Baker Street waiting for a client to come up the stairs.

The festive tidings of murder were not finished however.

Earl P. was still on the lam.

Then on a cozy evening it was announced that Earl P. had been tracked down in Canada by the Royal Canadian Mounted Police. The RCMP always get their man and they got Earl P., but only after a gun battle in which Earl P. was shot dead.

"I'm glad we didn't have anything to do with that," Parker said.

He was thinking of Bob Vanderland.

And then Bob came in. "Dead, huh?" he said. He stood gazing into the future. "This means that everything he's got is all mine, doesn't it?"

He was assured that it did.

"The place in the Hamptons, the Park Avenue penthouse, the Sprained Ankle estate in Vermont. Voodoo Island in Louisanna, Lucifers Mountain, Montana, the house in Kong Bay on Skull Island, Aztec Creek, Mexico, also Blood Lust Cove, the Isle of June, Bee Sting and Dead Fox where ever the hell they are?"

He stopped the list.

"Boomer," he said, "I'm too rich to be a cop."

He left the station.

"Come spring he'll come back," Parker said.

"Why should he do that?" Davy asked.

"He'll be miserable and he'll remember being happy here."

"What's going to make him miserable?"

"Money."

Whimsy, Davy said to himself, it'll be the death of all of us.

Outside on a bare branch winter tree an inquisitive crow cocked its head. A daemon of the old Salem, Massachusetts, witch-hunt school, it wondered what small town evil it could summon next.

Lightning Source UK Ltd.
Milton Keynes UK
UKOW05f1324031114

240998UK00001B/9/P

9 781781 487495